After Dying

Jesse Bier

ISBN 978-0-9964351-2-3

Cover art by Marlo Crosifisso

Cover design by Parker Beckley

Book layout and design by Mackenzie Cole

Edited by
B.J. Soloy
&
Myrrah Dubey

For information, email:
jesse.bier.mt@gmail.com

www.jessebier.blogspot.com

For Laure Bier

Chapters

Chapter 1

They found themselves in a kind of Terminal.

Mr. and Mrs. Cyrus Wells, in fishing regalia and orange life jackets, halted abruptly in the entrance way.

Cyrus Wells said, "This isn't so bad."

His wife Phoebe said, "Thank heavens, we're some place." She took off her life jacket, as did her husband. "This is still damp." She chafed herself. "And I'm cold."

"Of course, you're cold. You're dead. I'm dead. We drowned."

Now they turned and looked at three others behind them.

Phoebe Wells said, "I don't remember anybody else with us."

"Well, don't look at me," said Amos Kidderly. "I wasn't hiding in the crow's nest."

"It was a rowboat," Mr. Wells said. "On Lake Wah-hah-ma-tu-bah."

"Was that a resort—or a bad cough?" Kidderly asked. "Excuse me, I used to do that for a living: I was a stand-up comedian. Would you believe I died on—"

"—stage?" asked the third man in the group. He had a British accent and, in fact, was nattily dressed in 1894 Regent Street fashion.

"Hilarious," Amos Kidderly countered. "A little predictable, but very funny." He shifted from irony to triumph. "I happened to die on a hang glider, just north of Del Mar, California."

"Fact is," Cyrus Wells said, "we were in Minnesota."

The four looked now, as by common consent, at the last of their group, a pretty woman. She spoke to them with the slightest Spanish accent.

"I wasn't even in your country. I drove my car off the highway from Miraflores to Lima. An accident. I think." She acknowledged Mrs. Wells in particular. "That was Peru. *Very* south of the border."

"I'm not even from your hemisphere," said the gentleman with the marked, cultured British accent. Perhaps eyeing the woman from Peru, he added, "More's the pity. I don't believe I'm quite from your time either. I seem to be, perhaps, a hundred or so years out of it. 'Hang gliders' and 'cars'? *I* was thrown by a horse. The beast. I hit my jolly old head. Always knew it was the weakest part of me." He walked about during his remarks, coming in from the entrance way and making a little tour of the lounge section of the Terminal. He extended his hand to Mr. Wells, introducing himself. "W. Willie Downs," he said.

"Cyrus Wells," the Minnesotan responded. "My wife, Phoebe."

Willie Downs shook and held her hand just a perceptible extra second. "Charmed." He turned to Kidderly next. "How do you do?" he asked.

"I don't know exactly." But he shook the proffered hand. "Amos Kidderly. What's your 'W' for?"

"Oh, that's William. Redundant, actually." He turned to the Peruvian woman. "I'm 'Willie' to intimates."

She shook his hand, too. "You mean you were," she said. "We all were." Smiling, she introduced herself to the others as well as to him. "I was Maxine O'Gorman, painter."

"Beautiful," Willie Downs remarked.

"My paintings?" Maxine O'Gorman asked, though she recognized the old game and was smiling with radiant skepticism.

"Yourself," Downs replied.

"Oh oh," Amos Kidderly said.

Two figures stood immobile, swathed in bandages from head to toe behind a high reception counter in the middle of the Celestial Terminal. At that moment, they stirred themselves. The first figure—a male, to judge by bodily outline—spoke to his female complement.

"Here goes Intermediary Duty." To the group of five he said aloud, "You see us now. You're not startled at all."

Mrs. Phoebe Wells said, "Oh look—an invisible man and woman."

"No," her husband remarked, "I can see them. They're just bandaged, that's all."

Amos Kidderly added, "Maybe they were in an accident."

"Only in a larger sense," the first receptionist said: "contingency… I am G1. This is G2."

"G-men!" Kidderly exclaimed. "They're some kind of cops; Border patrol. Incredible. I don't even have a passport"—he felt his empty pockets—"or a wallet—"

Cyrus Wells felt his own empty pockets, wonderingly. "Man without a country?"

"Man without a world," Maxine O'Gorman suggested.

Phoebe Wells pinched herself. "I still feel my body, though."

"You don't require anything else," the figure G2 said. "We're here to furnish you with what you'll need," she finished with an ambiguous hand movement, "at last."

"Quite," Willie Downs observed, "but who are you, actually?"

G1 answered. "Corporealized black stars, perhaps. Intense spiral nebulae," he turned his fingers around, close to his head, indicating also his swathe of bandage, "compacted into helpful imitative form."

"What's he talking about?" Cyrus Wells asked.

Amos Kidderly answered, "I don't know—he don't say."

"The point is, for now," G2 said, "you're here. You're feeling surprisingly natural, relieved, at perfect ease. One of you is even—"

"—hungry," Phoebe Wells declared.

Now, in an alcove to their left, they spied a well-stocked buffet table.

But the Peruvian woman delayed them: "Why aren't there any more people?"

"Should there be?" G2 asked back cryptically.

"Well, doesn't everyone want continued life?" Phoebe Wells asked.

G1 replied, "Not necessarily."

"Not necessarily?" Willie Downs repeated.

"I can't believe this," Cyrus Wells said.

G1 said, "You will, sir: the Before, the Going-on-now… and the Afterwards. Meanwhile, you'll concede that most people—unlike yourselves—grow old?"

"They get tired," G2 added. "There comes a day when they don't care anymore, not really. They're used up."

"They give up," G1 went on. "They want it, deep in their hearts, to be all over. They crave—"

"—nothingness," G2 concluded, "peace, rest. Why, there are some who, even in the comparative sweetness of it, do not want to chance any more. Most people, one way or the other, have too long a life."

"Even among you five here," G1 said, "one or two of you glimpsed that truth?"

"Oh, the devil," Willie Downs said grudgingly, "personally, I… rather… presumed, once or twice…"

"Of course," G1 said.

"The question they might ask," G2 said confidentially to G1, "is: which is really worse, no life after death—or no death after life?" To the others, especially Mr. Downs, she said, "But you never got fully to such questions."

Willie Downs mused out loud: "Cut off in our prime, what?" He became apologetic, especially to the other two men. "Poor choice of words—castration and all that. Sorry."

Maxine O'Gorman asked, "We all died a premature death?"

Cyrus Wells was still reacting to Willie Downs' remark. "*He's* not premature, with a mind like that."

Amos Kidderly joined in. "I'd say, 'arrested' is more like it." He pointed to G1 and G2. "I *said* they were G-men."

Patiently Maxine O'Gorman defined her question. "I meant, has everybody here died an early, violent death?"

G2 pointed a long arm and finger at Amos Kidderly. "Not quite that one. Not so picturesque an end."

They all stared at him.

"You were not on a… hang glider?" Maxine asked.

"Yes, I was!" Amos answered. "Oh, hell. I didn't actually *crash*. Damn it… I had a heart attack in it."

Willie Downs exploded in sputtered laughter. Then, after a pause, he looked up thoughtfully, remembering something. "I once thought, as a growing lad, that a heart attack was a—hard attack. If," he added slyly, "you take my meaning."

"But we don't want your meaning," Cyrus Wells said. He looked steadily at G1 and G2. "Anyway, what's he doing here?"

"Yeah," Amos Kidderly was glad to second him, "from the 1890's?"

"Oh that?" G1 said. "Yesss."

"A slight… mistake," G2 said.

Cyrus Wells said, "That happens—*here*?"

"It's not usual procedure," G1 said. "But… it happens."

Kidderly, looking quickly at Maxine O'Gorman, said, "I don't mind a space mix-up. But a time warp like this," he glanced at Willie Downs, "is ridiculous."

"I beg your pardon," Downs said.

"You beg your pardon? Who asked for you anyhow? Which," Kidderly turned back to G1, "is exactly the point…"

"Now, now, gentlemen," G1 said.

"Just a minute," Amos said, "don't you call me a—! Wait a minute," he turned from slippage to seriousness, "I meant, don't call *him* a gentleman, not with all his snide allusions."

Cyrus Wells nodded vigorously. But Phoebe Wells came forward all at once and took Willie under the arm, "Well, he's dressed like a perfect gentleman, and he's got manners enough not to bite back at you two." To Willie Downs she said simply, "Come along," and moved off to the buffet with him.

"A repast?" Willie exclaimed. "Splendid!"

Cyrus Wells followed.

Maxine O'Gorman took a step after them but then halted. She indicated the sumptuous buffet and said to G1 and G2, "I don't believe I ever wanted to… devour the world. "

Amos Kidderly felt immediately susceptible to what she said. "That's funny—I understand you. Lots of times, all of a sudden, in an automat or a hamburger joint or even a nice restaurant, I'd get depressed by the sight of a person pushing a fork or spoon into their mouth."

"*His* mouth," G1 said.

"Why not *her* mouth?" G2 asked G1.

"It was just a question of antecedence."

"Indeed," G2 said.

Amos spoke to Maxine directly. "Stuffing ourselves—was it our essential act?"

"Something a little vulgar in it."

"Sure."

G2 addressed Amos: "Not cherry cheese cake, though." Then to Maxine: "Or a certain kind of tostada that Maria made at the old villa in San Isidro." Both Amos and Maxine, honor-bound somehow, nodded agreement. "Because there's another side, too."

"There always is," G1 said. "It's the main idea."

"Appetitiveness, for instance," G2 said. "Having a brief physical, material life for taste, miraculously."

"True," Amos agreed.

Maxine smiled but was serious in her confession. "Even if you were—as I was trying to be—a vegetarian."

"Except ," Amos said, holding up on objecting finger, "for the vegetables."

"Oh that," G1 said, "let me clear that up. They were nerveless. Had no feeling. Cut and winnowed grasses never cried. Bread was no embalmed corpse. The carrot was no tooth fixed in the jaw of the earth. And turnips *were* bloodless."

"Incredible," Amos said. "I'm glad, though."

"But—" Maxine started to object.

G2 cut her off politely. "Señora O'Gorman, you believe what you were going to say just now and what you will say later about cruelty, but you are also diverting us from yourself. You know very well that you had—" G2 glanced at Amos, who was cupping his ear to overhear—"he can't hear this—an appetitive side. Also sensuous, on occasion." Though stiff with pride, Maxine nodded just perceptibly. "Accordingly—" G2 made a graceful movement with her hand, momentarily putting Maxine either into or out of a spell.

"Yes," Maxine said, rousing herself, "perhaps I am a trifle... famished even." She moved now to the buffet.

About to follow her, Amos held up for another moment. He asked G1 confidentially, "How do you know that I, in particular, *wanted* to go on living, miraculously or otherwise?"

"It's the amount of your 'Incredibles' and 'Unbelieveables,' Mr. Kidderly. That reflexive, perpetual sense of wonder."

"You ought to listen to yourself sometime," G2 added.

"Never," Amos said. "that'd be a sentence worse than death… Oops! I can't believe that."

"There you go," G2 said.

And Amos Kidderly went off, to join the others. "Incredible," he said, "but very interesting." Arriving at the buffet, he asked, "Any cheese cake?"

The others had already partaken of delicacies. Now Maxine O'Gorman held aloft a tumbler of something, which Phoebe Wells also was sipping. "What is this?" she asked G2.

"Nectar ambrosium."

Phoebe said to her husband Cyrus, "I *knew* it. Nectarine juice!" She sipped some more of it, walking a little apart from the rest. Suddenly, as in a swift trance, she looked up. She was rapt, yet not absolutely certain of what she was going to do, and she spoke out the word loudly with a slight quaver in her voice. "Mama!?" she said.

G1 said, "Yes, you can make preliminary contact. Say what you want."

All alone, in her own circle of communication, Phoebe said: "Mama—just before the lake trip—just before I left down there—do you know… how much… apricots cost?"

When she moved away, some sort of temporary gravitational principle drew Cyrus to the spot. Meanwhile, at the buffet, Amos Kidderly found himself next to Willie Downs. "And what, in your extreme naivety," he asked Willie, "did you think *apple-plexy* was—too much fruit?" Willie Downs stared back fixedly at Amos, knowing him for an unabashed adversary.

Plate in hand, Cyrus Wells arrived at the place Phoebe had been in the middle of the Terminal. He, too, suddenly experienced a heads-up mental transport. "Dad?! I started taking pills, too. How about that? I still can't appreciate it… What? No: drowned. Phoebe, too. We got caught in the reeds. I think she was holding me down a lot." He began moving off. "One thing—I won't have to make out monthly checks anymore! Bills, checkbook, stamps—no more. Free…" He circled back to the buffet.

Next, Willie Downs sauntered to the center. He said, "Is that you, Ted? The only one I ever cared for truly, my brother, and you had to muck about in that Boorish War—and take a bullet. I've always wanted to tell you that. You bloody fool… What, me—what I did finally? Oh, what I always said I'd do. Marvelous time! Though I never had a sultry Negress"—Amos Kidderly was now approaching—"or a *really* long-limbed blond…" Willie moved off.

Amos, centered and transfixed in his turn, said: "Yep—heart failure. And I was taking Aerobics. You know, three points credit for swimming a couple of miles, or jogging four, or walking nine. I was regularly *driving* forty miles a day, cross-town L.A. All right, at even a quarter point per mile, that's at least fifty points a working week… Is Uncle Jake there? Uncle Jake, you told me everything but about Hollywood agents.

And why didn't you tell me," Amos began to move off, "to take care of the *dollars* and the *pennies* would take care of themselves—and if they didn't, that wouldn't matter?" He left, returning to the buffet.

Senora O'Gorman, who was really Senorita but was called the other because she was no longer a maiden of tender years, there being no relative title like Ms. (say, Senorissima, or Sss.) in her part of the world, approached the center of the Terminal but stopped short.

"I have nothing agrarian, medical, amorous, or commercial to talk about," she said to G1 and G2.

"Oh?"

"Also I am not a particularly public person."

Assuring or coaxing her, G1 said, "There are these moments others need not share…"

Advancing, Maxine O'Gorman said, "But I'm… perhaps—"

"—different," G2 said. "We know that. Still,…"

Centered now, Maxine confessed, "I never did understand funerals, for instance."

"Ah yes. Go on."

"I objected to all the bother, that's all. The being buried or cremated, having the grave tended afterwards or the ashes kept—or blown in the wind. Dead is dead, isn't it? *Wasn't* it? What difference between being chemically part of the earth or of the atmosphere around the earth?"

G2 said to G1, "She has a certain… cosmic sense."

G1 nodded to G2. Then he answered Maxine: "So that *survivors* would have a place, in the former case, to go."

No longer communing with, possibly, parents, Maxine addressed G1 and G2. "But why would you *need* to, if someone you loved is forever *in* you?"

"Ah," G1 said simply.

"*You* wouldn't need to," G2 answered Maxine. "For most of the rest, ceremony was very important. Perhaps all-important. It took the place of continuous feeling. You were—"

"—exceptional," G1 concluded.

"*That* was my problem?" Maxine asked.

"One of them."

"So, it was no accident on the highway between Miraflores and Lima?" She began to move off.

"The speed was no accident," G1 told her. "Only the accident was an accident."

"I see," Maxine said, going to rejoin the others, who now heard her last words: "I see, I understand."

Cyrus Wells put down his plate and took a step toward G1 and G2. Indicating the superlative Senorissima, he observed, "She speaks pretty good English."

G2 corrected him. "She speaks pretty good—Spanish. You are *hearing* in English."

"Then we're not talking the same language here?" Cyrus asked.

G2 asked G1 a swift, confidential question. "Does he have an extra insight now, do you suppose? Is he already starting to advance?"

"I can't be sure. I can't tell *every*thing," G1 answered her. To Cyrus he said, "No, it isn't the same, but everything comes out in your own language, Universal translator waves."

Cyrus turned about, stepping back toward the others. "Hey, that would have made a difference on earth. On any earth."

"No," G2 said, "not one bit."

"Oh, I said the wrong thing," Cyrus owned.

"Yes," G1 said, "but it doesn't matter and you no longer mind. And you'll keep on trying."

Suddenly, to their left, over hinged doors that they had not noticed in particular, a series of signal lights began to flash and blip.

"Here come some more truth-seekers," G2 announced.

"There will be a brief stasis," G1 told the group of five.

"You may overhear," G1 said to the group.

Chapter 2

Out of the door, on a sliding ramp, came a procession of assorted people who were moving across the Terminal behind the high reception counter. G1 and G2 turned about to give them brief audience. The first of the procession was a western rancher.

"I had a 'lectric fence 'round my pasture," he said unceremoniously. G1 and G2 nodded. "Now how come my horses—and jackassess—*knew* when the 'lectricity wasn't flowin', and they could lean on the fence and break through eventually?... I never did figure that one out... They smell it?"

"No," G1 said.

"Hear it hum, mebbe?"

"No," G2 said.

"What, then?"

"They went over to it periodically," G1 answered, "lingered there: close."

"If their skin hairs stood up," G2 explained, "they knew the fence was charged. Magnetism. Otherwise, they could just lean hard all they wanted to."

The rancher stared from G1 to G2, then he nodded, slowly and ponderously, with great satisfaction. He glided away now, disappearing eventually through another set of doors concealed behind a partition separating them from the Terminal entrance. A uniformed soldier was next.

The solder asked G1, "Did bullets... heat up in the air?"

Phoebe Wells exclaimed, "What a question!"

"No, listen," Cyrus said. "I wondered, too."

Amos Kidderly said, "It's a long shot, probably."

"As a matter of fact," G1 spoke to the audience behind as well as in front of him, "that is correct. The answer is—yes, somewhat—and those that go further, heat more."

The solder said thank you and moved gently on.

"Very nice," Amos commented. "And if that man was a continuous murderer—?"

G2 whirled around abruptly. "As it turns out," she said, "the man was a marksman—in target practice. Appearances to the contrary, he never actually shot at man or beast. In any case, through his long career this nagging little question of physics came to absorb and obsess him. He was capable of such disinterested objectivity, in and of itself. No mean matter, in all senses of the word."

"But *which* word," Amos asked, "mean or matter?"

"Mr. Kidderly?"

"Yes?"

"Kindly shut up."

"All right, all right. I swear."

G2 turned about again, to rejoin G1 in meeting a motel owner. The latter was a middle-aged woman with coarse greying hair and hard lines about her mouth.

She said, "I owned the Uniterian Motel."

"Unit*a*rian?" G1 asked.

"No, Unit*e*rian Motel. You see, that's it. Some people would think that I just misspelled it—that it was church property. But I hadn't—it was just what it said: fifteen units... And they were almost always filled up."

"Because people thought the place was cleaner and safer?"

"Yes! Maybe, after all, the Good Lord gave me the idea. *Did* He?"

"No," G2 replied.

The motel owner's face became discomposed. She sank in disconsolate shock, falling to her knees on the ramp as she began to move tearfully away.

Amos Kidderly said, "Do you know why—" but G2's accusatory arm was coming up—"just give me one more. Did you know why—not the chicken crossed the road—but why the Christian rode the cross? To get on the other side!" There was no reaction. "Esoteric joke. One of my main troubles. Never mind."

"Off, off!" cried G1.

"Who?" Amos asked, cowed, "me?"

G1 called after the departing motel owner, "Tears of delayed and convenient remorse? Off! Profuse lachrymosity? Off, off!"

"Oh," Amos said, relieved. "O.K., I'll calm down." The woman was gone, perhaps forever, and now two Neanderthal men, dressed in loin cloths and carrying clubs, approached G1 and G2. The second held the first and waved his club over him. "This is a dumb show," Amos said. He put his hands to his mouth and said "Sorry!" apologetically.

"The truth is," G1 said to G2, "we're explicitly set up for Speech. This is a prespeech pair. Another anachronism?"

G2 shrugged. "The Uncertainty Principle."

"No, no," G1 said in a suppressed voice. "It's the Imperfection Theory. That's different. You still have them mixed up, if I may say so."

"Sh," G2 put swathed finger to swathed lips. "not before others, please. And such lowlings. Sh."

"All right. Try your intuition and divination with these two. I'll mime and interpret for the others behind."

In effect G2 said to the second club-wielding Neanderthaler, "He complains that you want to brain him. Unfair. Unnerving. Unnecessary. Unintelligent. The kill-ee has family and friends who will catch up with and club down the kill-er. Mundane retribution. Mutual extermination. Missed civilization... Lower that club, unhand him. And stop grunting, both of you. I want you to move—move on!"

The Neanderthal men complied. As they disappeared, G1 turned and called after them. "Metaphorically, too! Don't either of you forget."

Now an automobilist in a camel's hair coat and cap approached the high counter.

G2 asked, "Question?" The automobilist took off his cap, smiled broadly and shook his head. "Demonstration?" the man shook his head again. G2 spoke to G1. "I've lost neurobiological contact. I don't know what he's intending to say."

"Guess, then," G1 advised.

Concentrating, G2 said, "He wants to make a statement. It has to do with a... memory."

"Perhaps he'll name the best auto he's ever driven," G1 ventured. "Or the highest speed he personally recorded? Say, at 2:05 A.M. on the interstate, ten miles south of Phoenix?"

"No," G2 was fixing her gaze and her mind on the man before them, "it's not a car itself, not a speed. I think—it's about a road, though—yes, a quiet secondary road in France"—the automobilist nodded now—"that's it—on a summer's afternoon."

Willie Downs interrupted eagerly. "It'll have to do with a woman."

The automobilist, cap in hand—looking into some far distance in his and G2's mind—spoke with slow, tongue-loosening languor. "A long straight road. Alone, in that roadster, on that road. The view in the rearview mirror—which I could look at, on that long straight uncrowded road, for maybe thirty or forty consecutive seconds. The trees—poplars—are like great green plumes, tall packed feathers, streaming on either side of the long straight—infinite—road... I can't forget that half-minute of—of—of inexpressible beauty and peace. That's all."

Willie Downs exclaimed, "Fancy that!"

The automobilist, who was the last one of the procession, made a bow to G2 and G1, replaced his cap, and then moved glidingly off. The group applauded delicately. The sliding ramp stopped very soon. The blipping lights above the ramp door went out. G1 and G2 turned around simultaneously, confronting the five once more, all of whom resumed a certain freedom of movement.

Chapter 3

Willie and Phoebe paired off briefly.

"Ever been on one of those charming French roads?" he asked her.

"No. But we got to Quebec once."

"I see."

"I didn't mean the city," Phoebe corrected. "I meant the province—especially the coast, fishing for salmon."

"You rather liked that?"

"Not at first." She gave it honest, direct thought. "Never, probably. But Cyrus seemed to have such a pas—" she was suddenly embarrassed by the word she had chosen, but proceeded—"passion for it, I started going along. I wasn't so lonely then."

"Oh."

Phoebe touched her hair, fluffed it. "That's why I was with him on that last lake, too."

"A storm broke, I suppose?"

"Nothing so... dramatic. What happened was, he broke his line but it caught for a moment on one of the rod loops and he managed to grasp the end of the line quickly and wrap it around his hand—you see, he had an enormous bass on the other end—and then he dropped the rod entirely and rushed to my part of the boat, and I stood up excited and he had that line wrapped around and cutting into his hand and—we just must have tipped the boat over."

"I daresay you couldn't swim?"

"Oh, yes, a little. But there were thick reeds there and a rotting log and—would you believe it? My *life* jacket sleeve got hooked through a forked branch and held me under... Well, I always said: Live now, Die later."

Cyrus Wells approached them just then. "Sure, you *said* it," he told her, "but did you ever really mean it?"

"Oh, but I'm not fibbing," she answered, "not the slightest bit. Besides, I don't believe we ever can here."

G1 said aloud, "Not telling a lie, or even a fib, and telling the whole truth are two different things." Then G1 bent again to some paperwork with G2, making entries, stamping, shuffling, marking. Nobody doubted they overheard—or underheard—everything.

Cyrus Wells answered unironically, "Say, that's deep."

Amos Kidderly, sitting at a little table near the buffet with Maxine O'Gorman, called over to him: "Well, remember, you're six feet under."

Ignoring Amos, Cyrus said to his wife, "You were a good cook, though, Phoebe, especially on trout."

Phoebe turned to look at her husband directly, though she did not quite round on him. "What do you mean, 'though'?" she asked.

Meanwhile, at their table, Amos spoke to Maxine. He pointed to G1 and said, "He gets a little proverbial sometimes, doesn't he?"

Was Maxine surprised at this turn of thought as such or at Amos' audacity? She said, "Perhaps you're right."

"What do you think G1 and G2 really stand for?"

Maxine shrugged, "What interests me is something else—the fact that they are in our own configured image, more or less."

"Maybe that's just not to startle us out of our wits," Amos said. "For me that would be a professional as well as personal calamity."

"Where did you work, may I ask?"

"I'm really from New York. But I was working at a place, a sort of nightclub, called The Comedy Shop, in L.A. It was just a month's engagement. And in that short time I had to go and get affected by California outdoor ideas and take up an offer from somebody at the club to try hang gliding one day at the coast."

"But you didn't crash?"

"I was actually strapped in, but I was on the ground yet when—" Amos began to drift into his memory— "we were on some gentle bluffs overlooking the sea and—" he was lost in his vision.

"Well," Maxine said gently, "then you had a fine last sight in your eyes at the end."

"What?" Amos roused himself.

"The view."

"Yes! The whole blue Pacific in my eyes! … That's me, though, the story of my life—never to know the real meaning of what was going on at the time, not even that last minute."

"You have many regrets?" Maxine asked.

"Not serious. Just what I said and the fact that I missed out on being… tall… dark… and more handsome than I am."

"Ah." Maxine smiled beautifully.

"And rich enough," Amos went on, encouraged, "moderately but distinctly successful and," he spoke straight to her, "much admired."

"Of course," Maxine said. It was a question whether her smile was more vast or scintillant. But it had a way of expanding the soul of the beholder, in all directions.

"And you, Maxine O'Gorman: that name. Let me guess. I once knew a Castilian Sephardi by the name of Don Levy—but he turned out to be Irish."

Now Maxine laughed. "Yes, my great grandfather was Irish. 'Maxine' shows the French influence in my country, in educated circles. It's all explainable." She laughed again.

Amos simply said, "I like it when you laugh." That made her turn almost demure. 'But you don't say much."

"I could never appreciate—please don't misunderstand; I believe I like you—but I could never appreciate immediate exchanges of confidence on earth. Or," she looked about her, "elsewhere."

"But why not talk to a sympathetic stranger once in a while?"

"But whatever was it that was so important to reveal, Mr. Kidderly?"

"Amos."

"Those exchanges that I happened to overhear in my life—on a bus, at a train station, in a plane—seemed only a kind of urgent… self-gossip. And then, Amos—"

"What?"

"I never quite trusted anyone to… tell anything *to*."

"His motive, you mean?"

"More than that," Maxine said. "I mean the terrible test, you see, of *his* understanding."

They fell silent. After the pause, Amos nodded several times.

"Did I pass?" he asked.

"What?"

"Did I pass the test just now?" She simply smiled at him beautifully. "So: not trusting a sympathetic stranger was one of *your* regrets? What else?"

"Oh, that I never visited Indonesia, Togoland, wherever that is exactly. Or even Tierra del Fuego. To live on earth, that little earth"—Willie Downs had excused himself from the Wellses and was approaching Amos and Maxine—"and not to have seen even most of it. It's too absurd."

With a gesture securing their permission to join them, Willie said, "Absurd? Outrageous! I happened to adore full-breasted women—in particular, I mean—and wanted great buxom women in Poland, the Ukraine, Tashkent. Well, I never got there."

"Listen to this!" Amos expostulated. "This retarded adolescent from 1899. Just listen."

G1 lifted his head from his desk work. "There's no affectation here, he's saying nothing at all for effect, he really *is* obsessed… Still, Mr. Downs?"

"Yes?"

"Your primary regret, please?"

"You mean about long-limbed—"

"Now, now, Willie," G1 prompted. "Think a moment. Get to it, concentrate."

"I ca-can't."

"Yes, you can," G2 said.

Willie sat or, rather, sagged down on a chair at the little table near the buffet. He said, "Not to have been—loved, actually."

"And—?" G2 asked further.

"And to l-love someone," Willie said. "But," he added immediately, "sexually, too. But," he acquiesced again, "past that, *through* it, to—*loving* someone." The Wellses had halted their private conversation and were listening from another little table where they had sat. "Is that why my thoughts, my testicular thoughts ran rampant," Willie concluded, "as far afield as Danzig, Odessa, Alma Ata?" He sank deep into himself.

"Me," Cyrus Wells was moved to commentary, "if I could have fished, say, Norway—those fjords. Or Chile—the trout in Lake Titicaca! And then: New Zealand. That's my regret."

"About the missed fishing?" Amos Kidderly asked. "How about the spectacular scenery?"

"What?" If Willie Downs was in himself, Cyrus Wells was far out of himself for a moment.

"The scenery, Mr. Wells?"

"Cy."

Amos sighed audibly. "Never mind the scenery, but—"

"No, I minded, in my way. You may not think so, but I minded."

"I was going to ask, what was another regret you had—down there?"

After a moment Cyrus answered, "Never did have a satisfactory, powerful pickup."

Now Willie roused himself fully. "Strange. I did. One, especially. I picked her up"—Amos groaned aloud, Cyrus simply stared incredulously—"in a hotel, in Mayfair, actually. Spiffily dressed woman. *Not* a whore, in fact. Well-spoken. Somewhat devout. Awfully good-looking, of course… I had her, on and off, that night—and she kept saying, 'Oh, my effing God!' over and over, at the appropriate times. It was enough," Willie ran a hand through his hair, "to convert a man… What a naked beauty she was!"

Amos stood up abruptly. He went to G1 and G2 at their console. "Listen. In some other places, this might be considered pornography. If you just hear him right."

"Not to mention blasphemy," G2 said.

"Actually," G1 said, "the man was in a torment."

"Some torment," Amos remarked.

"In point of fact," G1 said, "he's advancing along some other line. For the moment, he's a backslider."

"Well," Amos could not help himself, "he goes in for more than that… Anyhow, he's got a way of putting things that's—"

"—inflammatory?" G2 finished his thought. "And—the others can't hear now—you're worried that he may actually be inflaming the women, the O'Gorman woman in particular?"

"Because," G1 said, "you're all still somewhat corporeal here."

Pinching and squeezing his own arm, Amos agreed. "It certainly feels like it… Listen, I can't measure up to him. He's tall, dark—and too handsome. And so well-dressed. And: inflammatory. Is he going to be appealing here, too?"

"Yes."

"Hell." Amos looked back at the two little tables where the others sat. "To which one?"

"Both."

Amos socked a fist into a palm. "Why?" he asked. "And how's it going to work out finally? Where?" He looked all about the Terminal. "*Where*, for crying out loud? … Where are we, anyway? *When* are we. *Who* are we anymore?"

G1 said, "One at a time, Mr. Kidderly. And slowly. It's going on, it's clearing up, it's happening. Now: go back and rejoin them."

Amos did so. Willie was still musing aloud, "…a naked beauty."

Phoebe Wells spoke from where she sat directly next to G1. "Is there—there—love at *last* sight?"

"To some extent, always."

After a pause G2 said, "But was there—is there—love at *last* sight? That's the other question."

Phoebe was perhaps taken aback. She looked from Cyrus to Willie to Amos and then nowhere in particular. Momentarily she smoothed her hair. She fussed at her loose-fitting clothing. "But if God had wanted us naked, why did He give us clothes?" she asked. She was completely serious.

Nevertheless Amos said, "Ah-hah; she's getting down to earth." Almost at once he looked around confusedly and apologetically. "Well." He turned to Maxine. "Do—did—you ever have thoughts like that?"

"I think I can tell you something," Maxine decided.

"Yes!"

"The thought I entertained very often—"

"Yes?!"

"—had to do with skins, banana skins."

"Banana skins?" Amos visibly subsided in his seat.

"Recall that I was a painter. I wanted to paint—you won't laugh?"

"*Me*? No… I never did, you know. Others, of course; but not myself… Go on."

"I wanted to paint empty banana skins. To paint them empty but upright, or slightly folded at the peeled edges: but to give them life, *themselves*, a certain grace."

There was a sudden confidential exchange between G1 and G2, during which the others felt nothing but a momentary suspension of consciousness.

G1 said, "A certain gift of abstraction, I suppose. O'Gorman had another potential existence as a"—he picked up a printout—"theoretical scientist; also a mathematician. It reads out like that."

"Perhaps," G2 replied. "But all that's not the point just *now*. Don't you see? She wanted to give the *cover*, the exterior, of life its due. Why talk about her abstraction now, it's the reverse."

"No," G1 held fast. "It's realizing an ultimate, a foolish, but touchingly ideal view. Where's your—"

"—poetic sense? *Me?*"

Both of them cut off. They consulted their papers and forms with utmost attention. Their intense concentration was their distraction.

Amos asked Maxine, "Do you hear a kind of static sometimes?"

"A sort of crackling in the air." She made a motion vaguely in the direction of G1 and G2 at their high counter.

"Probably sunspots," Amos said. "Anyway, I was going to say, I understand you."

Maxine touched him on the hand. "I felt you would."

About to tell her something, Amos impetuously jumped up instead. He went back over to the central console. "A Confidence: can I claim a Confidence?" he asked. G1 and G2, recomposed, both nodded assent. "Can I tell her I love her now? Right now! I think I do."

"We know," G2 said.

"Then why not?"

"Too soon," G1 said. "Too strong and too soon."

"Your weakness was always poor timing," G2 said but, seeing Amos' sudden appalled look, added, "I meant, in love affairs."

"Oh." Amos was relieved. Then he said, "What am I saying 'oh' for? It's only an essential I kept missing out on?"

"Go back there," G2 coached. "You're singing your love song anyway."

Amos turned. "Will it do me any good? Will I be a fall guy here, too?"

"Kidderly," G1 said, almost impatient, "stop whining. Just… get on with it."

Sitting back down with Maxine, Amos resumed: "You know, I *did* understand a lot. I was even—well—kind of intelligent."

"Of course." Maxine's expression was amused but acceptant. "Pre-cocious?"

"No," Amos answered quickly, "I was Jewish right from the start."

"What?"

"Never mind, just a wisecrack… Actually, it was no laughing matter being smart. Can I call you Max?"

"All right. Why?"

Amos glanced at G1 and G2. "To keep my distance—and timing."

"All right—Amos… But wasn't man the intelligent animal? That's why he survived, dominated."

"Hold it, wait a second. It was survival of the fit, not the fittest. The fittest were the really bright and sensitive, and the rest dominated *them*—pushed them to adjustment, or to clowning, or to art. That's my theory."

"You're playing with words a trifle."

"I always did… What do *you* think?"

"Why, I rather like that."

"What?"

"You're genuinely asking me what I think," Maxine said.

"So?"

"I think it's a question of power, isn't it? Or of numbers, which may be the same thing. But perhaps," she looked toward the high console, "things are worked out differently on other worlds?"

G1 and G2 shook their heads. Amos and the other three were looking at them also.

"No perfection anywhere?" Maxine asked.

"Like getting banana skins to stand up straight?" G1 asked back. "Only in your head."

"Anyway, no perfect miracles in this part of the cosmos," G2 added.

"But come to think of it," Cyrus Wells remarked, "we had enough minor little miracles on earth, didn't we?"

Willie Downs was enthusiastic in remembrance. "The water closet! Featherbeds. Rubber… products."

Phoebe Wells recalled, "Electric egg beaters. Blenders!"

"Easels," Maxine admitted fondly. "Turpentine. Acrylic paints."

Amos glumly added, "Canned laughter."

"I think maybe," Cyrus drew out another thought, "they were… working on… powdered water." Amos shot him a look of consternation but decided that Cyrus was serious.

"And not only inventions," Willie said, 'including cars and hang gliders, but the creatures we had about us. Fine hounds! And—I bear no grudges—thoroughbred horses."

"Birds," Phoebe said. Then she shivered in a recollection: "And bats."

"Butterflies," Maxine said.

"Mosquitoes," Amos contributed.

"Gnats, worms," Cyrus said, "and something… something about centipedes—"

"Well, how about a praying mantis," Amos remembered, "unbelievable. Or the whatchamacallit, manta ray? Anyhow, what an earth!"

They fell wonderingly silent, nodding in unison.

After a moment Willie said, "By the way, old chaps, since I *had* thoughts about such things down there and the ol' spinning top we were on and all that, at odd moments—"

"You can say that again," Amos said.

"—at odd moments," Willie repeated, though he looked askance at Amos and now directed himself specifically to G1 and G2, "how did the earth jolly well—happen? Just asking."

G1 answered, "Solarus Mediocre swept through debris in a motion that captured your planets and made for their elliptical orbits."

"Did that also flatten the poles?" Phoebe Wells asked.

"Don't mention them," Amos said and then, indicating Willie Downs, added, "he's already spoken about the full-bosomed kind. You'll confuse him, anatomically and geographically."

Willie approached Amos. "See here," he said, "why do you insult me?"

Chapter 4

Amos glanced at G1 and G2 and then replied. "Because I hate and despise and—envy—everything you stand for."

Willie Downs straightened his shoulders. "Oh. Well, that makes sense." He retired some steps, walking with squared shoulders and muttering something to himself, as he took a turn or two of self-satisfaction.

"And the moon," Maxine asked G1, "was it coeval with the earth?"

"Or swirled off it?" Phoebe asked.

Willie was back in the group. "Out of the Pacific perhaps?"

"Look who's had his intellectual side?" Amos remarked.

"Yes," Willie returned. "Did you, by chance, have a physical side?"

"Are you casting aspersions on my manhood?"

"If the shoe fits—"

"Shoe—fits? What kind of a pervert were you?"

"Please," Cyrus Wells said, "there are ladies present. One of them was talking."

"Did the moon come later or was it—"

"Co-evil," Amos put in: "guilt by association?"

"Mr. Kidderly, by now you should be resisting yourself better," G1 said, picking up a graph of something and turning to G2. "His brain scan seems to be all right. Hmm."

G2 addressed Maxine. "The answer to your question is, yes, more or less co-existent… Ms. O'Gorman, we are going to send you somewhere temporarily. Because of your interest in the moon."

"I'm interested, too!" Amos said.

"Not as long as she," G2 said. "Or psychogenically."

"How's that?"

"The menstrual cycle. Moon was derived from your Greek, 'mensus,' remember. And the filling and full moon symbolized pregnant women. And the moon reflects the sun's glory—myth and astronomy, not politics. And the moon has phases. So: fecundity, dependence, changeableness all account for the profound interest."

G1 relinquished the graph he was studying for another note. "She had recurrent 'moonlight periods' in her landscapes…"

Pointing to the Terminal entrance, which was also, of course, an exit, G2 gave a direction to Maxine O'Gorman. "If you will just go back through that areaway and take the first door to your right, please? The Planetarial Theater; retroactive movies."

Maxine left. There was a long pause, with glances after her, prolonged to stares from the others, wonderings, divagations. Willie Downs came back to the subject.

"You positively mean it didn't come from the Pacific Ocean?" he asked G1.

"Of course."

"Personally," Phoebe Wells declared, "*I* never cared that much for any moon—no matter what you said about *her*," she indicated the exit and departed Maxine. "Wasn't the moon lifeless? That was the main thing that put me off. *She* never had any children. I bet."

"You did, of course," G1 said. "Two children; one Caesarian."

"Ah-hah," G2 exclaimed mildly. "The moon… ripped out of the Pacific." She wrote a note.

Phoebe grappled with the issue. "But even the first natural childbirth was quite painful? Why? Why on earth all the basic pain?"

"To treasure the offspring of such clear suffering." G1 turned to G2 for an aside. "Am I beginning to sound sententious, ever so much?"

"Quite!"

"A simple yes or no would do. You needn't be so—emphatic."

But Phoebe Wells went on. "Those offspring—squawking as they come in and going on crying right through infancy. Why did babies cry so much?"

"Babies cry," Amos said, "because—" he reached for his joke.

"—because," Cyrus tried it, "they knew—if they talked—nobody would listen."

"I say, that's jolly good," Willie Downs said.

Before softly stunned Amos could say anything, Phoebe approached the high central desk. "Can I claim a Confidence?" she asked.

"Yes."

"I was disappointed in my children at every age. Maybe it was me. If you don't love your children, enough—or if you do, too much?—you'll ruin them either way. And it's *your* fault, never theirs for not reacting properly or predictably." She looked up quickly. "Mama, why didn't you tell me? Oh… you didn't know in time either." Facing back to G1 and G2, she said: "Honestly, if I'd known more, I never would have bothered… with it… or most things."

"Perhaps," G1 responded. "But you didn't want this to be a Confidence—not really, Mrs. Wells."

"No?"

"No. Say it out now. To *him*."

Phoebe turned and walked directly back to Cyrus Wells.

"I never really wanted children. I never even wanted to be married."

"Feeb!"

"And will you stop—please please please *stop*—calling me Feeb?"

Cyrus was speechless. Then, at last, he asked, "You didn't want to be married?"

"Well, *stay* married, I suppose. Oh Cyrus, how I tried to be a good, even athletic wife. But you didn't *need* me; maybe someone else, but not me."

"How do you know?"

"I know. You had your intense fishing, for instance. Maybe I even grew jealous of it. Anyway, you had it." She appealed to the rest of them. "If he'd been sentenced to flail his arms hours on end in the middle of flowing water and walk up and down mile after mile all day long to no place in particular, he'd have called it cruel and unusual punishment. But, on his own, it was pure pleasure."

G1 lifted his head from the console desk. "It was," he affirmed.

Maxine glided quietly back to the group from the entrance-exit areaway. She sat and listened.

Phoebe continued. "And I didn't care that much for the great outdoors. Trees! All right. So what?"

Amos agreed, nodding emphatically. "Sure. Still," he said. "the weekend before… Del Mar, I was in Sequoia Park. I—I pocketed a redwood acorn. Nobody was looking. I just took it. There were a lot of them laying there."

"Lying," G1 said.

"No, I'm telling the truth… I want everybody to know that I experienced one whole week—my last!—of childish but anxious guilt for that act. I'm genuinely sorry."

"All right," G2 said.

"Trees," Cyrus meditated. "They live, grow, die." To Amos he said, "They get diseases, you know. I never got over finding a thing like that out. And flowers have sex." He glanced, with Amos, at Willie Downs, who made no remark.

"Now he doesn't say anything," Amos said.

It was Phoebe who spoke, after peering at Amos. "You weren't crazy about nature?"

Amos shook his head.

Maxine joined in. "Then you wouldn't have liked most of Peru… Still, I admit there was cruelty in nature. Not only predatory." She looked at Cyrus. "Even, or especially, his fishing."

"No, m'am," Cyrus said simply. "Actually I used barbless hooks, especially on my number 18 flies. I generally caught the trout on their lips, where they're nerveless.

Then I brought them in, carefully slipped out the hook, and let most of them go."

G1 said, "He was virtually training them to be wary." Maxine was impressed, contrite. Yet G1 said to her, "Yes, don't be *too* quick in judgment, it's your weakness."

Phoebe wandered over to the buffet, chose a dish of cucumbers, and then seated herself at a table where she discovered a deck of cards. She was just in a mood to play something and delicately fork a slice of cucumber now and then.

Willie sauntered over. "May I?" Phoebe nodded for him to sit by her. "Solitaire? Hmm. How about two-handed rummy?"

"My favorite," Phoebe said and re-gathered the cards.

They reshuffled and played.

Amos sat next to Maxine. "Good," he whispered.

Maxine gave a quick low laugh. "You don't know if he likes her really."

Amos kept his voice down. "What do *you* think of *him*?"

"He's very handsome," Maxine answered without guile, "*hermoso*."

"Oh-oh," Amos said; "when that Spanish starts coming through…"

Phoebe exclaimed about some play of the cards, "There're the five of hearts!"

Some distance away, Cyrus wouldn't let that pass. "*Are*?" he asked.

Gallantly, Willie Downs defended his partner. "You might say, it's plural."

"*It's* one card," Cyrus said.

Phoebe went on playing. But after a moment she said, "That was another thing. Not only wouldn't you play cards with me, you made fun of me sometimes."

"Teasing," Cyrus replied.

"That's for you to say and me to know," Phoebe replied. "You thought you were more intelligent."

After the slightest hesitation Cyrus asked, "Wasn't I?"

"Maybe, but I was smarter. Oh, I know how that sounds, but it's true. I would have *done* more with you brains." She held up a moment, remembering something. "Expending yourself on sugar cubes!"

"Sugar cubes?" Willie Downs was struck by that. He resumed playing, but listened hard, as the rest did.

"We were at another lake once," Phoebe explained. "Crystal clear. Unfishable: they'd scatter at any sight of you. After a while, we just picnicked. Then he," she stopped playing again temporarily, out of memorial acknowledgment to Cyrus—"I suppose he was *smart*, for what he wanted—he noticed the box of sugar cubes in the picnic basket. He just took one suddenly. What he did was, he wedged a hook with a salmon egg on it inside that sugar cube, and then he went to the deep end of the lake near us, and dropped that in."

"Weighted like that," Cyrus joined in remembrance, almost reciting it, "it sank to the bottom softly, dissolving. All that was left, at the bottom, was a salmon egg, covering a hook, just lying there—never having startled anybody on the way down."

Phoebe had resumed her game with Willie. "He eventually caught a six-pound lake trout."

"*Eight* pounds," Cyrus said.

"Capital!" Willie Downs congratulated him. "I mean, sir, not only the fish in question, but the concept. Ingenious."

"Yes," Maxine O'Gorman said, looking with a sort of fixed wonder at Cyrus.

"But don't you believe," Phoebe insisted, "that it was an absolute waste of one's powers to be thinking about and doing things like that?... When any fool in an empty setting like that—"

"What do you mean?" Amos Kidderly asked.

"Gin," Phoebe said to Willie. "I win!" She stood up abruptly, taking a step or so toward G1 and G2. "That day, alone there, I would have wanted him to—expend his energies otherwise. I wanted, in the middle of nowhere, after we ate, to be—ravished." She touched her hair, clothes, arms in quick succession, becoming self-conscious. "I seem to be warming up."

"Is it the humidity or," Cyrus asked, cocking his head toward Willie, "the humanity?"

Amos spoke suppressedly to Maxine: "Is he going to fight for her? Maybe she's not worth it."

G1 said to Phoebe, "You would like a change of costumes. For the reasons just indicated." He pointed to the exit areaway. "To the left, out there. The Cosmical Wardroom. All your size. Take what you want."

Phoebe left.

Cyrus went to the buffet. He took a goblet of nectar and walked over to the central console. "Can I ask a funny question?"

"No!" Amos Kidderly said.

G1 said, "Yes."

"Of course, fish eat. For all I know," Cyrus said, "they suck sugar. But I'll be damned," he said, waving his goblet, "if I ever knew whether fish *drink*."

"Yes, they do," G1 said.

"Oh," Willie Downs said, "are we allowed pertinent and impertinent questions again? Splendid. Say, was all that going on in Roman times really true? Orgies and all the rest? Between—who was it—*Calingula* and *Lascivious*?"

"For crying out loud," Cyrus said. He had glanced at Maxine.

"Why?" G1 asked him. "Because the subject is unpronounceable—

"—or unmentionable?" G2 asked. Not waiting to hear, G2 turned to Willie with her answer: "True: all you ask about was true."

"My word!"

"And how about *my* word?" Amos asked. "I dropped out of college afterwards, but I'd like to know the right answers to the A.C.T. exam I took in 1951. The vocabulary section, I'm especially sensitive to that. Like—something's coming back—like the difference between 'debasement' and 'abasement'—"

"See here," Willie Downs said.

G1 answered, "Imposed and self-imposed. Here, you may have this," G1 picked up a test-and-answer booklet from his desktop and handed it down to Amos, who approached and took it and returned to the table he shared with Maxine and leafed through the booklet.

Maxine asked G1 and G2, "Am I so much more morbid than everybody else? Why is it I retain a certain terrible and, I think, typical picture of earth?"

G2 said, "Don't judge *yourself* so peremptorily either. Just tell us the picture."

"It's one of my professor of music, who played in a quintet—*who kept on playing* in a quintet one particular day: the day of a Lima/square massacre during a fascist revolution. No, it was a leftist revolution. Well, leftist fascist. Well, that part is not important."

Amos put aside his booklet. "Not important?"

"What affects me," Maxine said quietly, "is that I see and hear him *going on playing*—Mozart!—and I hear and now also see that littered square. You understand? For me, that was earth."

"Go on," G2 said with gentle persuasion. "There's something else, to increase the perspective."

"Half of the people in that square were our Indians, *peons* who had no politics at all. None whatsoever! You see, they came down from their impoverished beautiful mountains to live in their shanty towns of Lima, feasting abundantly on the garbage cans of the city and roaming the streets—and squares." She shuddered somewhat.

"Go on," G2 urged: "a little further—a personal divigation."

"Some of them, of course, were luckier—hired help paid next to nothing, but sheltered and fed after a fashion. Nobody was more loyal, more virtuous than our Indian maid, Maria. And now I could suddenly weep—or weep again!—for certain small scenes etched on my mind."

G1 said, "They will not be terrible, only poignant."

"That's even more terrible sometimes," G2 said.

"Yes," G1 said.

Maxine recalled Maria. "She was up every morning at six to make our breakfast, and she cleaned up after supper as late as 9:30 or ten every night. She slept in an alcove we had far away upstairs."

"A sort of slave," Amos said.

Maxine recoiled. "Don't say it."

Cyrus Wells said, "It wasn't your fault, you were six."

"When I grew up," Maxine concluded, "I managed to take her places with me—on a drive, shopping in town… I discovered she was eager to see a football game—soccer?—and took her to a match, which I detested then as I do now." Willie Downs harrumphed. "We finally married her off—to one of those players." Maxine shook her head ruefully. "Poor thing, it worked out badly."

After a pause, Willie said, "We understand. But, I say, you needn't have attacked sports. A matter of social compensation—blood and circuses and all that. You rather missed the point of it. And perhaps a good deal else."

"Wait a minute," Amos stood up, "you're speaking of the woman—"

"He has a case, I'm afraid," Maxine said directly. "I was beginning to miss the point, the reason, for many things. Even for most paintings, including classics. I found myself questioning *every*thing, too much."

"Maybe," Cyrus Wells volunteered, "you were just on the verge of something else."

Before Maxine could acknowledge the remark, Phoebe Wells returned. Dressed now in soft, flaring calf-length boots beneath her bare thighs, with a wide *décolleté* tunic sheath above, she was splendid.

Willie Downs said, "I say."

To Maxine or to Cyrus—or to himself—Amos said, "She's worth it!"

Phoebe reseated herself at her card table, where Willie rejoined her, spilling the cards once or twice before dealing effectively. Cyrus spoke to G1 and G2.

"I was going to ask, didn't people go on leading lives"—he indicated, in turn, Maxine, Amos, Willie, himself, and Phoebe—"painting, clowning, whoring, insurance and fishing, and *cooking*—that they wanted to lead, in the end? Didn't they?"

"No. Not necessarily," G1 replied.

G2 pointed to Maxine. "Didn't you hear what she just described?… How could any life be the one you wanted to lead set against a background like that?"

"I meant," Cyrus spoke hesitantly but doggedly, "with the world as it is, what with the compromises you had to make, you got the life—out of all the possibilities ahead of just you in particular—the life that you could get most conveniently—and that, therefore, you… wanted?"

"Hey, I thought he was pretty superficial," Amos said.

G1 made a hand gesture figuratively brushing Amos away. "Very good, Mr. Wells. Nevertheless, tell us one or two of your own disappointments, some characteristic frustration—apart from not getting to Norway and the fjords."

"And," Cyrus could not stifle the memory, "losing the biggest grayling in North America one day when—"

"Yes, skip that," G1 directed.

At her table Phoebe Wells cried, "Gin!" and Willie Downs said, "I don't quite understand your mode of scoring—or your alcoholic vocabulary."

"That's all right," Amos commented, "just leave her in charge."

"Why, thank you," Phoebe said to Amos.

Cyrus was answering G1. "I… never… did get the cuckoo clock in the hallway synchronized with the electric alarm in the bedroom."

"I take it back," Amos said, "he's profoundly depthless."

"And shaving every day!" Cyrus went on.

Phoebe glanced up from re-dealt cards. "Why on earth didn't you raise a beard?"

"Matter of fact, I thought you objected."

"Not that much."

"Well," Cyrus said, "you certainly fooled me. Say, is that the *only* way you fooled me?"

Amos Kidderly felt both sides of his face. "I used electric razors all my life. Humdingers!"

"Marvelous," Willie said, folding his cards for a moment. "So there was progress, of a sort."

"Yes," Maxine said, "Remington razors and ammunition."

"I'm not sure you can mention brand names up here," Cyrus thought out loud. "Just say, fiberglass and graphite rods."

"And how about the Pill?" Phoebe said. "For my daughter, anyway. And nail polish—and nail shields they were perfecting."

Amos stroked his face again. "The thing is, I never did learn to shave any other way!" He looked about. "They better have 120 volts or one of those little transformers or—it is true, isn't it, that the hair keeps on growing for a while?"

"Only shy men wore beards in our era," Maxine observed. "Why would you—?"

"I was shy," Amos explained. "I was just overcoming it all the time… Anyhow, there were getting to be bearded comedians by the time I left. That might have made me popular."

"Weren't you?"

"No. I wanted to be great and popular. Instead, I was just good and moderately well-known."

"That must have been what you *really* wanted," Cyrus Wells observed.

"I was just too cerebral." Amos said.

"See?" Cyrus said.

"Well," his wife put down her cards, "I had the opposite problem. I never thought anything out; I never *thought* long enough. One of *my* biggest disappointments is that I never had a fixed philosophy."

"*Fixed*?" Cyrus said. "you never had a new or a whole one to begin with."

"That's what she said," Amos intervened. "Stay away from oblique punning, you're singing my song. And she'll thank you to stay out of her *medulla obligato*."

"And out of me, out of my entire life!" Phoebe said abruptly, strenuously. "Don't think I didn't hear what you said toward the start here—or I just heard it?—about my pulling you under the lake, back down there. How could you? I was simply… holding on for a moment, by the reeds—"

"Phoebe, you're almost a hypocrite." Cyrus turned to G1. "Can that be so—here?"

"Only self-deception. Quite transitory."

Willie Downs sat back in his chair. "Self-deceit: by George, that may have been it!" Simultaneously, he gazed into his past and spoke to the others. "My most disappointing memory was a self-deceiving *de-virgination* that—don't guffaw—truly shocked me."

Amos appealed to G1. "Is he putting us on?"

"No," G1 said, "no."

"Shocked," Willie elaborated his memory, "having taken such a thick-thighed, well-built gal to bed—*her* bed, by Jove—hearing her protest the way they did, flinging herself all about, both of us deliciously naked. 'Oh no, oh no!' she said, mounting *me*, protesting over and over 'no!' with *me* supine and startled underneath, and *she* bursting herself at length, if you don't mind my saying so, and crying 'What have you done to me, wicked man?' although it was not quite finished yet, and then it was, very shortly, for both of us, certainly for me, and she—turning or pirouetting off—still saying 'What have you done to me?' Well," Willie looked at the others, "I've never been so disappointed in human nature before or since. Can you all believe that, to this very moment, I have been secretly—and in a decided way, morally—outraged by her attitude, by the deceit she was capable of in the very throes of her time? But," he asked G1, "it was self-deception?"

"There," G1 replied, "it was both."

After a pause Maxine said, "But life held plain deceit and fraud, too, surely."

"Almost never plain," G1 said.

"What's behind it," G2 prodded, "what do you wish to ask?"

"Did Picasso de—?"

"What, what?" Amos prompted.

"—depend on fraud?"

"I thought you were going to say, de-virginate his models," Amos said, "that's why they're fractured, or something. Max, what a letdown!"

G1 answered her, "Yes and no. Since most people could no longer tell the difference between cartoons and art, he gave them both, sometimes alternatively and sometimes simultaneously."

"*That's* why he was the greatest artist of the twentieth century?" Maxine asked.

Suddenly, in *sotto voce*, G2 said to G1, "*Twentieth* century?"

G1 quickly sifted through some sort of printouts. "Ah—let's see for sure—four billion, 600 million, 300 thousand, seven ought-ought. I think it's in the ought-ought." They bent their swathed heads together.

Amos patted Maxine's shoulder, "Don't take it so hard," he said.

"Oh," Maxine said, "I was coming to certain recognitions, including the fact that almost everything was imposture. For me, it probably *was* time to d—"

Cyrus Wells broke in unexpectedly. "No, no!" He spoke to the others. "She just needed a sort of barbless brush."

Maxine considered him or the proposition for a moment. "I don't think so. You see, for me painting had become a blend of passionate work and tyrannical pleasure, far too urgent. It had become even—well—painful, to bring something to conclusion."

"Like—birth?" Phoebe wondered aloud.

"Perhaps," Maxine said, "I only felt demonic sometimes, and at other times quite empty. And, I confess, I felt a need for fame—*while I despised it all*. And there was the growing obsession of those curious banana skins I mentioned. I—I—" she rose, touching her throat. "I have gone on so, haven't I? I feel quite thirsty. Perhaps some of that nectar…?" She went to the buffet.

Phoebe addressed G1 and G2. "Are we all, each of us, going to go on—and on—*here*? Will there be something else, or—"

"Or what was the use of dying?" Amos asked. "Excuse me, I wasn't just being funny. I'm beginning to afford not to."

G1 said, "Actually you all died many times before dying. You had lots of practice."

"Try to remember," G2 said; "there's a distinct possibility that you can recall or sense the very first case—memory traces are left in the brain—if you truly concentrate. Remember dying away from lovely hydraulic/pneumatic/oxygenate/shock-proof perfect equilibrium at the very moment of uterine ejection?"

"Birth was death?" Willie Downs asked. "Oh. Yes, of course."

"Furthermore, you kept on dying," G1 added, "through all the phases of your life… In your young adulthood, for instance, didn't there come a moment when, suddenly, you remembered the boy or girl you once were—the child who had been you but *no longer was?*"

"And didn't that keep happening," G2 proposed, "seeing your past self, a dreamed self—you and yet not you, as in another life? Asking yourself then, was that young woman, or young man, *me*? And to go on and on feeling your distant selves at once familiar and yet gone—"

"—buried away from you," G1 finished, "as in another life. You see—a whole series of deaths and lives and deaths again. Dying wasn't unusual."

"But," Maxine asked, "now: what's ahead?"

"Ah," G1 said.

"Why the mystery," Cyrus asked, "what's the future?"

Alarmed, Amos Kidderly exclaimed, "Holy smoke! Is there a future. I mean, after this—" he peered all about, genuinely appalled, "after this TERMINAL?!"

As if a frozen probe had gone into their brains, they all experienced a sudden Absolute Zero of consciousness. It was only a second, however.

Cyrus Wells recovered first. "No, there's something more, something else. Don't you *feel* it?" He asked G1 and G2, "What's ahead?"

G2 shrugged. "We're not God."

"Not even the two of you?" Cyrus asked.

"Hey," Amos said, "*I'll* take the funny lines. Oh-oh," he pointed to the left door behind the light console, "there go those lights and that blipping again!"

Both G1 and G2 turned abruptly around. Another procession, led by a Hunter, was approaching. The Hunter put his hand inside his jacket suddenly.

"He's searching for something!" Cyrus Wells said.

Chapter 5

"A gun!" Amos cried.

Phoebe Wells said, "But why?"

"Up here?" Willie Downs asked.

"Nonsense," Maxine O'Gorman decided. "Look."

In fact, the Hunter had drawn out a pocket calculator. He arrived before G1 and G2, and he put his question.

"Was hunting—by the year 1990—in the North American area—in either the province Alberta or the state of Montana—venison and elk meat—less expensive than going to market? Include the cost of freezer."

"And transportation," G1 added and jotted something on a memo pad. "That's gas and oil, and depreciation on the four-wheel drive. And let's not forget about amortizing the guns."

"*Amortizing* the guns?" G2 said. "You are deviating into morbid wit."

G1 glanced up and almost turned his head around. "It must be Mr. Kidderly's fault. There's a certain amount of reciprocation here." He turned back to the Hunter. "It used to cost you exactly one point seven times as much as supermarket beef."

"Can you beat that?" the Hunter remarked, departing on the moving ramp.

"Yes," G1 called after him: "you had a great deal of fresh air. And you definitely helped to cull the herds."

A Hindu woman approached G1 and G2 next. But behind them Willie Downs felt inspired.

"I say," he asked Amos Kidderly, "did you ever eat chocolate mousse?"

"And vanilla antelope? I know." He peered at Willie Downs challengingly. "I—er—remember the name, but can't place the face."

The Hindu woman halted before G1 and G2. "Will I ever be released from immortality?" she asked.

The group of five exchanged elbow pokes and looks.

"Yes," G1 said.

"Now?" the Hindu woman asked, looking shyly hopeful.

"Now," G2 said. "No more transmigrating for you. You're done, finished. You may be atomized."

Grasping and kissing G2's hand, the Hindu woman cried, "Oh—thank God!" and moved off in happy radiance.

Half turning, G1 addressed the group before the next pair of the ramp procession arrived. "You understand? There is a kind of oblivion for those who finally and truly want it…"

"Then this is Heaven?" Phoebe Wells asked quickly.

"We didn't quite say that," G2 said over a shoulder.

"This is just what it—is," G1 said. "For now—a parade of questions, protests, declarations. And for you, other wheres, other whens."

Now two Ancient Greeks, newer versions of the Neanderthals, stopped before the high desk.

"Are they," Amos referred to them, "in our experience, or we in theirs?"

"What difference does it make?" G1 answered, turning back fully to the pair on the ramp behind.

"He's a crypto-guardian, if you ask me," Amos said aloud. "Should we trust them?"

"We have no choice for the moment," Maxine observed. "Shall we listen? I rather think we're supposed to."

The First Greek was grappled on the arm by the other. He spoke up to G1 and G2.

"All right, we're out of the caves. We're not clubbing one another, all the time. We just capture each other all over the place. I'm his serf. That makes me a Hades of a lot better off?"

The Second Greek shook the First. "You wretch! You're in an advanced state of ancient classical culture. But you complain!" To G1 and G2 he repeated, "He whines and complains! Tell him something."

"You don't feel glad to be alive?" G1 asked the First.

"Not excessively."

"Hear that?" the Second asked, exasperated. "Between servile and treacherous, what I have here by the scruff of the neck," he held him as he spoke, "is the ideal Golden Mean ingrate."

"Take your hands off him," G1 ordered. The Second Greek was surprised but complied. "Did you capture him yourself?"

"Not exactly. We're at a considerably higher level than that. The wretch cost me four and a half drachmas."

"Answer the question,' G1 asked the First Greek. "Is your fondest wish to be free?"

"My fondest? Of course not. It is," he said, turning around and grasping the Second by *his* neck, "to take *him* by the scruff of his neck and make him *my* serf." He loosened his hold.

"So," G1 said, "three thousand years to move from mutual extermination to mutual enslavement. Conceptually speaking. It's not quite—ultimate, is it?"

"Not ultimate?" the Greeks cried in chorus.

"Turning the tables I can conceive of," said the First, "but there's something else, something higher?"

"Get along," G1 directed, pointing to the exit, as the ramp began moving again. "Get moving. Find it. Philosophize, discuss, develop—grow *on*, grow on!"

They moved away and off, as a Cross-Country Skier approached the central desk.

Amos Kidderly could not help addressing the others. "Did you get the symbolism?"

"It was O.K.," Cyrus said, in all probability genuinely impressed.

"Don't be rude, Amos," Willie Downs said.

"Amos? *We're* on a first-name basis?" Amos asked.

But G2 was conducting another, supercedent interview. "You have a Question?" she asked the Skier, who shook his head. "Protest?" He shook his head again. "Declaration?"

The Skier nodded. He smiled at G1 and he smiled at G2, and then he looked into a private middle distance. "I was in a sunlit gap in the woods. Ahead of me, all of a sudden, while I was looking that way, heavy pure white snow cascaded off a middle branch of a great spruce tree, and when the branch swayed back up, the force made all the rest of the snow explode out into the blue air."

Everybody gently applauded. The Skier left, as a City Man approached.

"I appreciated that," Cyrus said.

"He had a fine pictorial sense," Maxine said.

"A trifle military, perhaps," Willie commented.

"Oh, come on," Amos countered, "105 millimeter—snowballs?"

"I liked 'cascaded' and 'blue air' especially," Phoebe said: "lovely."

The City Man was halted in front of G1 and G2. "What about speed-reading?" he asked just like that.

Amos called up to G1 and G2, "Let me answer that," and they let him. To the City Man he said, "It's *very* important if you're hunched up too much in a roller coaster at 95 miles an hour and have to read the 'Duck your head' sign."

Willie Downs said, "Sometimes slowness counts, you know. As in sex—"

"Keep calm," Cyrus Wells said.

"Hey," the City Man spoke to G1. "I'm in a hurry."

"You're—what?" G1 asked. "*Here?*"

"I think I heard right," G2 seconded G1, "even with this gauze over these

33

presumable ears. Off with you—"

G1 pointed to the exit, as the movable ramp speeded and the City Man fell suddenly sideways to his knees, according to the law of physics and his changing understanding. "Out, out," G1 said, "*fast!*"

The blipping and humming went out, and the ramp carried the City Man away and stopped sharply.

Chapter 6

"Damn," Cyrus said.

"Precisely," Willie took it up. "I say, has he just been sent to a further corner of—Hell?"

"Further?" Amos asked. "I think this is only a mid-level jail. They have movies here, wardrobe, food…"

"And perhaps rooms," Willie guessed.

"Well, I'd still like something less confining," Phoebe declared. To G1 and G2, who had turned about again, she said, "This is a nice place to visit, but I wouldn't want to live here."

"I'm afraid we have to mark that down, on her record," G1 said, and he wrote something quickly with his finger.

"Ah-huh, they keep saying 'record,' did you hear?" Amos asked his companions. To G1 and G2 he said, "Mrs. Wells was just being funny, in her way."

"Why not—cancel it?" G2 prompted G1. "Weak satire, not premeditated cliché-mongering, it seems to me. She doesn't have to be stigmatized for all time."

G1 erased his previous mark with the heel of his hand.

To Amos, Phoebe said, "Thank you!" To everybody she said, "Did you hear that little phrase, 'for all time'? Did you hear that?… But do they know about my being so conscientious—and mainly good—on earth?"

"Were you?" Maxine asked.

Phoebe thought hard. "Well, I never meant to harm anyone."

Willie said, "Not the same thing, old girl." He answered her injured look quickly. "Just an expression, that last, nothing personal… I rather suppose none of us here deliberately hurt anybody."

G1 pantomimed binoculars with coiled taped hands. "Are those wings," was the question for G2, "budding out of their shoulder blades?"

Who could tell if G2 smiled? Or if, indeed, there was a face behind the swathing?

After a pause there was only another question, put to everybody. "Was there no one in life that you crossed or mortified at all?"

A long moment of self-communion.

"My parents," Maxine admitted. "By being a painter. And not to have married Colonel Juan Luis Felipe Ramon-y-Calderos de Fortunato."

"How old were you?" Amos asked.

"Eighteen."

"Sure. Young and scared. You thought they were marrying you to the whole regiment."

Maxine appreciated the joke. But then she said, "It was not truly a laughing matter. My parents never recovered from it. I deeply regret that… And you?"

Amos replied, "Dropping out of college: that hurt my mother. And bombing on the Ed Sullivan Show: that hurt my father." Maxine reacted to "bombing," so that Amos added quickly, "No, I wasn't a terrorist; it was just an expression for failing big on the stage… Also, I never treated my kid sister, 'Sahndra,' right. They should never have named her that maybe, it gave her airs from the start. Anyhow, I wasn't nice enough to her, ever. And now it's too late."

"Well," G1 commented, "*that* part, at least, is hell."

Willie Downs was also confessional. "And I—did not—love any woman back. Not ever," he was remembering very particularly, "especially one on my mind. I was a sort of charming, casual blackguard." He looked at each of the others in turn, his gaze resting finally on Amos, who resisted wisecrack and comment.

"And evidently," Cyrus said, "I shouldn't have married Feeb—er—Phoebe. I hurt *her*."

"And probably, deep down, all the while, I hurt you," Phoebe concluded. "I certainly did *me*."

They all reflected.

"So," Amos summed up, "it turns out that we all fundamentally crossed or hurt *some*body close to us, by doing or not doing something… And another thing: it's gone on, sort of, since we've been here, even—bickering around, shifting allegiances, exchanging little hostilities. Two splitting up," he indicated the Wellses, "nobody else coming together yet—or ever?"

Phoebe ventured, "Then maybe we *are* going to…?"

"Suppose," Willie had another thought, "we are not going to Hell but—"

"—*coming* from there?" Maxine caught his meaning.

"You mean," Cyrus asked, "that the earth was hell, even for relatively good people down there?"

"*Down* there," Amos mused: "hmm."

Willie elaborated. "Perhaps there were—various circles of it, different privileged levels—"

"—but all somehow unfulfilled, or worse," Maxine said.

"But that would mean we *were* bad," Phoebe speculated. "I don't feel I was… Wait. Maybe as a child?"

Cyrus shook his head. "No. We lived on the same street; I know you were O.K. Normal."

"I can't be sure," Phoebe said.

G1 glanced at G2, who nodded, and said, "You two may leave. Also for Retro Movies: two private showings. Out there," he pointed to the exit, "turn right, go on."

After the Wellses departed, Amos came forward. "Listen," he said to G1 and G2, "can I go sometime?"

"You don't have to," G2 said. "Your whole life is at instant recall."

"Is that a fact? Or a criticism?"

"*We'll* ask the personal questions, Amos," G2 said. "Now, tell us something. What do you consider *your* main problem was down there?"

"The main problem I had? That's easy: I was never ready for anything, at the *time* for it. Not even for kindergarten, for crying out loud—which I did a lot. And not for being a teenager either, not until I was in the *next* decade. I've been consistently behind! And just about now I've been feeling, say, twenty-three; but I'm *forty*-three. See? If anything, it's been getting worse… Looking back over the whole thing, I was never ready for any of the stages of my life."

"Yes," G2 said. "And for you, in particular, something more—"

"Right, something else. *Me*, the real me, I wasn't ever ready for the stage. I'm not really funny, in my heart. I was always serious, even too serious. Take school. Say, the seventh grade, in shop. We made wooden dog letter holders, big Great Danes on either side. I whittled and filed mine down to a toy poodle on one side and a Chihuahua on the other. They couldn't hold my mother's Green Stamps, never mind her letters and bills. I took it hard. Then high school. In French I knew all the tenses but couldn't speak a word; I still can't say '*chambre á coucher*' right. Freudian foreshadowing. But I took it seriously. And those crazy problems later on in College Algebra: if a bird is flying back and forth between two trains, approaching each other at forty and fifty miles an hour respectively, and if they are 315 miles apart, and if the bird is traveling at twenty-five between train A and train B, *and* it's two hours past Greenwich—are we in England or Connecticut?—and *what* kind of a bird was it that would do a thing like that?" There was no reaction from the others. "You can laugh, all right. But I went crazy trying to figure the homework out… Only later, in that and practically everything else, did I see that *it wasn't so important*. Don't get me wrong: I loved living— only it was so untimely and off-center." Amos stroked his throat. "I think I'll have a shot of ambrosia." He went to the buffet.

"Well," Maxine said, "perhaps you just ought to be grateful that life didn't make you a carpenter."

"Or a Frenchman," Willie added. "Or a railway engineer."

"Yeah," Amos agreed. "Or a mathematician. The things I either could or should never have been!... How about you two?"

"A nurse," Maxine said swiftly.

Willie said, "A barrister."

Amos made a tortuous arm movement. "One of those long swooping kinds you slide down?" Willie straightened a moment but then smiled. "A little levity there," Amos said. "How about a weight lifter? A sky diver?"

Maxine said, "A box office ticket girl."

"A hor—" Willie drew out his word, "—te-cul-tur-ist."

All at once two children, looking in miniature like Phoebe and Cyrus, entered from the areaway. They were scolding one another.

"Shame on you, Cyrus Wells," the girl said.

The boy said, "Go jump in the lake, Phoebe... Feeb, Feeb!"

"I'll *tell*," she said.

"Tell who?" he asked, looking at the others. "They all *know* by now."

Confidentially G2 asked G1, "What happened?"

"They were supposed to review, not reduce. A slight error."

"The Principle of Uncertainty?"

"No, no," G1 said, "just Imperfection again. You keep getting all that mixed up."

"Perhaps. But it's not as serious as getting *them* mixed up."

"Well, we're not supreme, G2. This is Intermediary, remember? I daresay even on supreme levels—never mind. You two," he called to the boy and girl, "off you go. Grow back up. Out there and right away."

The girl and boy scurried off.

Maxine said, "Nun," resuming the conversation with Amos and Willie, who looked at her perplexed. "A nun with a habit," she said.

"How ambiguous can you get?" Amos asked Willie with loud feigned confidentiality. "And you?"

Phoebe and Cyrus Wells re-entered.

"A police inspector," Willie replied.

"Terrific."

"What are we playing?" Phoebe wanted to know.

"Personal impossibilities. Incredible alternatives."

Cyrus said at once, "An expert plumber."

"A gymnast," Phoebe joined in.

"Our school principal," Cyrus said.

"No actual personalities," Maxine said with authority. She did not know whose authority. "Only abstracts."

"A psychiatrist," Cyrus continued.

Phoebe said, "Chorus girl. I can't dance at all."

Then Cyrus said, "An insurance man."

Nobody said anything.

Then somebody said, "But he *was*—"

"—an insurance—"

"—man," somebody else said.

"Yes, I remember," Cyrus said, "but deep inside me... deep... it was im—"

"—possible," Maxine said. She said to everybody, "He's right, you know."

Amos sauntered over to Willie. "Could you have been a telegrapher, ol' chap?" Willie nodded. "Take a stellargram to my father, wherever he is. 'Dear Pop—Send $250 right away—Stranded—God knows where. Stop. Need one-way ticket fast to—to *where*?"

Willie shook his head. "It's no use, the games turn serious... I thought we were warding off real memories, and then—"

"Oh-oh, you've got another one of your own that you want to get off your hirsute chest? Go ahead," Amos put his hands over his eyes, "I'm not listening."

"Well, as a matter of fact, I recall this particular woman—"

Cyrus said, "Not again," turning his back.

"She was a countess, actually. She said, 'Dear Boy, you're so vivid. If you go on doing as much as you say, I'll be in heav—heav-heaven!'"

"Well—?" Maxine inquired.

Amos uncovered his eyes. "Don't ask."

"—*was* she?" asked Phoebe.

Willie was surprised at them. "But that's not the point. The point is—was—that I suddenly understood, even in my success—or *hers*—that I was nothing more than a juvenile stallion. It was that 'Dear *Boy*.' I was thirty-eight at the time, you see. It was a shattering revelation. Ruined my future, actually."

"How's that?" Cyrus asked.

"Well, a view like that—oh, you mean specifically? Truth is, I began not to consummate success myself half the time. Unnerving."

"So," Cyrus reflected, "in the end, sex is used up faster than fishing?"

G1 sent a question down. "Does that satisfy you a great deal about your own sublimation?"

"What?"

"You heard," G2 said.

Willie spoke up for Cyrus. "But he's quite right, you know. In the end, I failed all the time, in sex. As to love, I had no idea. They *were* different. But—how to tell the difference?"

"Simple," G2 replied.

G1 looked quickly at G2. "Simple?"

"Simple." G2 turned from G1 to Willie. "If you wanted women, Mr. Downs, it was sex, successful or not. If you wanted one woman, it was love—and that's successful, no matter what."

"The worst thing, then, probably," Maxine theorized, "is not even not to be loved, but—"

"—simply," G2 said, "not to love."

"Oh lord," Willie said, "that's me!... I think I should like a sweet." He went back to the buffet.

Cyrus expressed an idea he had, pointing at G2 and making a shapely silhouette motion with his hands. "I think she's a—a—she," he said. "I think there's a difference of opinion according to which one's talking."

"Very interesting," Maxine said.

Phoebe said, "I wish I could see their faces."

"Not if we just found them out," Amos suggested, "they'd have a wounded look." He added in a mild manner "That's why they've got the bandages."

"Now, you see, *that* I find funny," Maxine said, laughing softly. "And you put it in such a gentle way. Amos, you're a nice person."

"I wish you wouldn't say that."

"Why on earth not?"

"Because every time some woman said that, she was letting me down easy."

"But I value you, Amos."

"You do?"

"I do."

Quickly, from the high console-pulpit, G1 said, "I do *not* pronounce you married."

"What did he say?" Maxine asked Amos.

"Nothing. He's kidding. For once."

Phoebe glanced from Amos and Maxine to G1 and G2, asking, "*Do* opposites attract?"

"Wrong question," G1 answered.

"Everything attracts," G2 said, "at one time or another. The question is, what holds?"

"What holds?" Phoebe repeated.

"Complementariness," G1 said.

Willie had wandered back toward her and heard. "Very well," he said to G1 and then to Phoebe. "When you walk, there are sparks where your fleshy kneecaps barely touch. Your hair exhales a witchery of scent. And a man could suicidally hurl himself down your infinite cleavage."

"Infinite?" Phoebe said. "Oh!"

G1 said, "I meant complement with an *e*."

"Compatibility," G2 explained. "Complementary hands, left and right. Compatible mittens and mates. Two together. One of the secrets of the universe is—dualism." Looking quickly at G1, G2 turned her certainty into query: "*Two* of the secrets…?"

"Hear that?" Cyrus said to Phoebe. "And you a married woman wanting to be single again."

"You're the one who doesn't hear well. I didn't exactly say I wanted to be single again always; I said I wanted a divorce. They're two different things."

"All right. But why, basically?"

"Because you've been unsatisfying even in my dreams, Cyrus. In all sorts of ways, including your spurning *me* sometimes."

Amos said to Willie, "Psychological reversal. Subconscious transformation."

"Egad, you don't suppose she's a secret nymphomaniac?"

"Just a nymph. Cool it."

Maxine said to Willie, "You've been the sensualist, we know that, but you were starting to feel continent, abstemious—?"

"—continent?" Amos took it up. "He comes from another world entirely, another time even. Another frame of mind he keeps sliding back into."

"Well," Maxine said, "you yourself just punned again. Evidently our old saying in South America is true: you can't step out of your shadow."

"I'll show you," Amos said, improvising a comic dance, trying to step out of his shadow. "Wait a minute. We don't *have* a shadow here."

Cyrus was berating Phoebe. "You were so worried, back there, about your children—when they'd marry, *if* they'd marry, whether they'd *stay* married—and now you want—"

"My reward," Phoebe said, "for stamina. I want to catch the next plane, preferably with someone else."

"Plane?" Amos interrupted. Now he extended his arms like wings for the benefit of G1 and G2. "Plain plane—or plane of existence?"

G1 answered, "Both."

"I might have known," Amos said.

Cyrus had turned directly to G2. "Listen, am I responsible for how I act in her dreams?"

"Yes and no," G2 replied.

"How's that?" Cyrus asked.

"If by some deficiency in yourself you occasion her need to see you in a certain light. A wrong view of hers objectively, but a right one subjectively."

"And that's *more* real?"

"Just *as* real," G2 said.

Amos said to no one in particular: "Get all that?—'both,' 'yes and no,' and 'just as'—that's what it takes to be God."

"Poor Cy," Maxine said.

Willie and Amos exchanged looks.

"I have a completely hypothetical but fetching question," Willie said to Amos, "to cut across this present discussion."

"Yes?"

"Will a husband forgive his unfaithful wife if she testifies afterwards to his sexual superiority?"

Phoebe was put off, even angered by Willie Downs. "How could you put it like that—even theoretically—in reverse like that?"

"Sorry, nothing personal," Willie said. For Amos he revised himself. "Allow me to rephrase. Not would he forgive her, would he believe her?"

Amos let it fall away, appraising Willie. Presently he asked, "How did you get like this? Spoiled childhood, wealthy father, inherited title: second Coxcomb of Sussex?"

"Rather not. No money, actually, or title."

Despite himself, Amos was interested in the matter. "How did you make a living then? Gambling, I suppose."

"Somewhat, old scout. And—well—larceny." To the others as well as Amos, he said, "Come now, it was a larcenous world, wasn't it? Stupid Boer War, for example, fought for diamonds actually." He shrugged. "Well, I had my own war."

"And a scam?" Amos asked eagerly. "A con-game."

"Rather. The same one, in fact, over and over. I made an irregular living by for-aying into a prominent jewelry district—Edinburgh, York, Southampton—and pur-chasing a moderately expensive ring or bracelet by cheque—always on Saturday or just before Bank Holiday—and then proceeding across the street and selling it—or try-ing to sell it—to a competitor… The two establishments would inevitably consult, behind my back; surreptitious messengers, telephone calls, very subdued—and then the police would invariably arrive. And I'd be hauled off to the bailey. Yes, I spent a total of twenty-three days in prison, all told, on separate 'scams'—each day or so suc-ceeded by the discovery on the next legal workday that, indeed, there *were* sufficient funds, in my quite un-fictitious account, to cover the cheque."

"Cheque!" Amos said. "You know from the way he says it, it's spelled q-u-e. Abso-lutely delicious."

"Fancy," Willie said, "that I never once, in all those occasions, had to go to court, actually. They never chanced the publicity, further trouble, scandal. There was always a large apologetic settlement. In fact, a living!"

"Incredible," Amos said.

"They didn't have insurance dicks yet," Cyrus commented. To Willie he said, "Still, I have to give you credit."

"Odd expression, that." Willie smiled benevolently. "Beyond the aesthetic dimension, however, was indeed the cash factor—life and liberty, as you Americans say in other irrelevant connections. I mean, I too needed to be free."

"Except for three weeks and two days," Maxine observed. To G1 and G2 she said, "Was it all—"glancing in turn at Phoebe, Cyrus, Amos, and Willie—"home, row boat, stage, hotel room, studio—a prison?"

G1 said, "Yes—" and G2 said, "—and no."

"Ah," Amos said. "Hey, that's another one: 'Ah.' Dignified Aloof. Very knowing. I'm catching on."

Ignoring Amos, G1 asked Maxine a question that answered her own. "Were you not, while living, wrapped in the soft prison of embodiment and materialization?"

"Ribs like bars," G2 suddenly conveyed poetry, "the heart beating a delirious drum, and thieving touch locked within the skin."

"I say," Willie responded, "that's rather stimulating."

"Take it easy," Cyrus said.

Maxine had a meditative thought. "I believed, back then, that what I'd miss most of all after dying—if you could put it that way—would be the feel of each new spring. Heavenly." She went in and out of momentary rapture and memory. "I don't feel spring or any other breezes here."

"We're indoors," Cyrus said.

"Isn't there any air conditioning?" Phoebe wondered.

"Is there any—air?" Amos asked. Everybody stood stock-still for a moment. Amos spoke. "This is known as a pregnant pause."

"Are *you* being suggestive?" Willie asked Amos.

"As a matter of fact, no. Well, maybe. I don't know. Not all the time. Like—"

"I say, old chap, may I tell you a formal joke?"

"Just once."

"What is the difference between frustration and utter frustration?"

Amos pondered. "This must be so old it's new. Let's see: frustration is—is—"

"—is the first time you discover that you can't do it the second time."

"Oh. Yeah." Amos took Willie by the arm and moved apart with him. "And utter frustration is—is—"

"—the second time you find out you can't do it the first time!"

Amos clapped Willie on the shoulder. "*Very* good. I hate to jolly well admit it."

They strolled back to the others.

Along with the women, Cyrus had heard. "But his joke," he said to G1 and G2, "was telling the truth."

"How do you know?" Maxine asked him.

"My masculine intuition."

"Yes, it's true!" Willie exclaimed. "Yes, yes! This body," he turned to Maxine: "wind on my face—that's safe enough. It might have done for you. But I—I—was such a vigorous man, don't y' know?—to become so unsure of *that*. O, the evil nature of decline!"

"Well, I was on blood pressure medication," Cyrus said companionably.

"I started wearing half-glasses," Maxine admitted.

"I *stopped* contraceptive care," Phoebe said. "Mind, you, I felt—invigorations yet—even all the more—but I was finally past… the worry."

"I was having these palpitations, especially on the stage," Amos said.

"Decay!" Willie cried. "Too early—at any age. My opinion. The world was, finally, not well done."

"There were those spring breezes," Maxine recalled.

"And hurricanes," Willie countered.

"And earthquakes of childbirth," Phoebe said.

"And storms of war—beatings—massacres—" Cyrus said.

"Yes, the revolutionary square…" Maxine said.

Amos suddenly resisted the conversation. "Hold it, everybody. I seem to remember soft summer rains in the Catskills and fleecy clouds—and sometimes we had peace, too—and people could laugh, joke—"

"It was *not* my world," Maxine decided.

"In general?" Amos asked. "Or is phony art still getting to you? Never mind, don't answer."

Suddenly playing the part of an impresario, Amos led a brief minstrel interlude, shuffling a soft-shoe introduction each time he signaled someone of the group to make a joke or simply to express and release himself. Willie was the first to understand the self-generating charade.

"A person—how do you say?—cracked up her—car? Yes—outside of the Museum of Modern Art in downtown Lima. Before the wrecker came, they gave her first prize in Contemporary Sculpture."

Amos smiled broadly, He nodded to Cyrus.

"We couldn't get average Minneapolis youth into the great outdoors, no matter what program we tried. Imagine!"

"You don't have to imagine what's real," Phoebe objected. "Besides, don't I remember a local columnist who disagreed, calling all that the Bucolic Plague?... I was a city person, myself."

"Still," Maxine asked, "what kind of a hectic, citified world was it becoming with fast and junk foods?"

"It was getting to be," Cyrus said, "that, with all the mono-sodium-glutamates and what-all they put in just a quick hamburger, when they said 'to go,' they meant you, not the burger."

Amos now comically conducted them like a vocal orchestra, calling on each for notes of discontent or simple bafflement. He pointed his invisible baton at Maxine.

"I could never understand why they made it so difficult, so impossible, to open up a package of American dry cereal. Really!"

Phoebe said, "Will someone explain to me who made—and who wore—woolen undershirts with *short* sleeves?"

"I'm still back with horses," Willie admitted: "their tails always swishing like that as if, yes, they were wagging like big dogs. But they were shooing off those beastly flies, not showing their happiness to see you. I should never have trusted them."

Maxine came in again. "I did enjoy little unspoiled dogs, however, on the same planet with us. I didn't like the barking dogs in our Indian villages, though. And I didn't like—I never understood—Indians—or anyone else—with tattoos, of all things. And, then, everybody else starting primitive, show-off self-mutilation."

Amos stopped conducting and spoke in his own turn. "Something *I* couldn't appreciate on earth: I never understood—I was frightened by—circus clowns. Why?"

Willie said, "Sepulchral white faces, old chap."

"Big sad eyes," Maxine said.

"Great glum mouth," Phoebe added.

"The joke was—death," Cyrus finished.

Amos was struck. "Of course!"

G1 intervened speculatively, "Solarial earth was quite difficult for man."

"How about woman?" Phoebe asked, impertinent but compelled.

"I trust the expression was short for man*kind*," G2 said.

"Remember," Amos touched Phoebe's shoulder briefly, "women are kinder than men."

"Oh," Phoebe said appreciatively.

"Men, women," Cyrus said, "we weren't most of it, not even half of it; maybe shouldn't have been any of it... How about the fish and the animals? They lived there, too."

"And flowers," Maxine said, laughingly, "who had sex."

"Curious," Willie meditated again. "What was even more perplexing was hermaphrodites." He glanced up at G1 and G2. "By the way, nothing double *there*."

G1 seemed taken aback. "Er... yes. Of course. The *general* rule is compatible duality." He recovered himself. "We had to have some hermaphroditism so that we would not assume dualism too monistically." G2 elaborately clapped her swathed, muffled hands. "I can sense your applause," G1 said and bowed.

"I thought I was mocking you," G2 said, "but I no longer know."

"Thank you," G1 said. "Strangely, I believe I was right." To Willie, G1 said, "What else?"

"Oh nothing really. I simply could not, *deeply*, understand hermaphrodites in the same world with me, that's all."

"Could you understand grass, trees?" Cyrus asked. "What plain up and down miracles! Could you even describe them?"

"I daresay, as we saw everything else in nature around us," Willie replied, "from *our* point of view." He extended and crooked his arms. "The *limbs* of the tree, for example."

Standing next to Phoebe as Amos was, Amos turned to her, almost touching her bodily parts as he proceeded in enumeration. "The *brow* of a hill. *Eye* of a storm. *Mouth* of a river. *Neck* of land. *Arms* of a lake. Excuse me," he said, reddening, remembering her accident. He looked down and trailed off, "*Shank* of evening, *foot* of a mountain…"

"It's all right," Phoebe murmured, almost tenderly.

"Matter of fact, the last time I was stream fishing—" Cyrus said.

Phoebe changed at once. "We don't want to hear about fishing and fish!" she cried. "How come you exactly remembered an eight-pound lake trout once more than any baby's weight?" She stalked off some paces.

"Matter of fact, I wasn't going to talk about fishing when I mentioned the last time I was stream fishing. I was going to say it was along about dusk. I was in a high stream by a long stand of yellow'd trees. I thought they were early-turning larches. But they weren't. They were—diseased pine. All right? Trees got sick!"

Amos wagged a finger upwards. "What a goddamn thing."

"You weren't religious?" Maxine asked, more bemused than critical.

But Amos rounded on her, though not heavily. "I meant to ask you—did you ever do still lifes?"

"Yesss."

"And how about Mosaics?"

"Why… no."

"Then you weren't religious either. Sorry, Max; you were out of line." He turned to G1 and G2. "Let me ask something, I always wanted to… How about what Cyrus was leading up to? How about—disease?"

"The circle of predation," G1 answered. "Instead of the big on the small, the small on the big."

Maxine prodded Amos. "Ask about cancer."

"Yeah," Amos said to G1, "and cancer: the worst of all."

"Also, purely theoretically, of course," G2 replied, "the best of all. Oh yes: cancer's a surplus, not a defect of life. Cells growing instead of dying. Too much of a good thing. The body autonomously cloning itself, perhaps. Or excess immunology against viral saboteurs... But too much... Mid-earth man will conquer all the diseases proper, to go on dying of a weariness or an imperfect too muchness, of one kind or another."

"That's a hell of an answer," Amos said.

G1 and G2 both shrugged. They said nothing further.

"Well," Maxine said to Amos, "anyway I enjoyed your braveness."

"'Bravery' actually," Amos said: "I mean, the word. Notice how their Translator Waves aren't absolutely right either... But you admire moral courage?" Maxine nodded emphatically. "Emotional conviction?" She nodded again. "Good!"

"But then," Maxine indicated to Willie, "he's still handsome. And," she inclined her head just perceptibly toward Cyrus, "I think more and more of *him*. Well, don't be so utterly surprised. You have not exactly remained proof against other charms." She gestured at Cyrus' wife, who had slipped into a private reverie.

"That's just because I'm basically a city person too, like Phoebe—"

Phoebe came out of her reverie, answering to her name. "—Nightingale."

"Your maiden name?" Amos asked. Demurely, Phoebe nodded. "It's an unexpected but lovely cognomen," Amos said.

Willie overheard. "That's *not* the way to go about it," he said. He shook his head briefly but woefully. "I could teach you a thing or—"

Cyrus stalked heavily to the buffet. "I think I'll take a grain of salt. With all of this."

Glancing at his back, Amos wondered aloud, "Is he my past—or future—rival? Don't answer," he said to G1.

"Am I the only one suddenly hungry?" Cyrus asked sociably.

G2 turned quickly to G1, lifting a hand and outstretched finger, remembering and signaling something. The ramp began to slide once more, making a slight whirring noise, and the lights over the left door blipped and hummed softly on again. "Lions get suddenly hungry," G2 said or recalled, and turned about face with G1.

A black Kenyan Ranger approached the high desk along the ramp.

Amos called up. "Wait!"

Chapter 7

G2 turned halfway around to look at Amos Kidderly.

"Can I try with you… a little," Amos asked. "up there?"

G1 said to G2, "It's time," and G2 said to Amos, "Come along."

Amos went up a little staircase and joined G1 and G2. G1 stepped momentarily aside from cover of the console, revealing a kind of ballerina skirt; G2 also made room, stepping apart to reveal a sort of codpiece, then turned back again with G1. All three concentrated on the Ranger's interrogation.

"Why do lions sometimes eat zebra," the Ranger asked," and other times lie around perfectly peaceful right next to them?"

"Perhaps you don't quite mean *that* question," G1 suggested.

The Ranger tried again. "Why do the *zebras* act unconcerned when zebra-eating lions are lolling about right next to them?"

"That may be it," G1 said.

"No," G2 said, "it's the first question, or answer, that determines the second question, or answer—"

G1, G2, and the Ranger looked at Amos.

"How come—er—the lions pounce on the zebras sometimes," Amos stated, "and *other* times not? In other words, it's a yes-and-no proposition. Or—both. Or—just as: Ah." He stared at G1. "It's a question, obviously, of… hunger. Of course. Yes. Lions are, otherwise, quite placid. Lazy. Even sleepy. Three-whole-fourths of the time. Hanging around. Literally: on the lower sturdy branches of acacia trees." Now he looked at G2. "For shade and rest. Or in the tall grass. Right by the zebras. *They* don't mind; the lion isn't hungry then. But by and by he gets his appetite back. And he… sees the zebra differently. The thing is," Amos now faced the Ranger directly, "he's noticed before that the zebra is kind of a *horse*—with stripes—or, he figures, *bars*: he thinks the zebra-horse is in jail, inside a safe cage. What's the use? But then his hunger releases a chemical, and that affects a certain substance in the retina of his eye, called—"

"—tapetum," G1 said.

"—tapetum, and he can no longer distinguish the color black, *the color of the bars.* Staring at the zebras, he thinks all of a sudden—they're 'out'—and he jumps them!"

"And the zebras, simultaneously, sense the lion's abrupt appetite—" said the acceptant Ranger.

"—or hear his stomach growl—"

"—and prance off. Marvelous," the Ranger said. "I knew there was *some* explanation. Thank you. Very much!" He gave a quick, smart salute and moved off, as an old yarmulked Jew, Goldberg, approached along the ramp.

"Oh, it was nothing," Amos called after the Ranger. To G2 he said, "I was guessing."

G2 said, "It was inspired."

"Was it *true*?"

"With fewer and fewer lions and zebra left," said G1, "they may never know. Until then, it's true."

Goldberg was halted before the console and spoke directly to Amos Kidderly. "It's a long story, you got maybe a minute?... Before the train crash I met my enemy, Levin, in the second car. The second-class car, the second car, what difference? Anyhow, 'Nu,' I said, 'so where are you going?' He says, 'Cracow.' Naturally I tell him, 'You say that because you want me to believe you're going to Warsaw. But I happen to know that you are going to Warsaw. So: why are you lying at me?!" He paused. "And *this* man— this liar, this long-life hypocrite—is dying after the train crash—and me, too—he's on a patch of grass next to me in a field by the tracks, and I hear him say to God—praying yet!—'I was a good Jew. Better than Goldberg. In my *heart.*' The chutzpah! And I saw him—before he died, before I died—his fingers trembling with death, fear even— point, *point* to his heart—as if he believed it!... The last ten years he hardly came to Temple, not even on Passover." Goldberg looked blank, waiting.

"Ask already!" G2 said.

"Wasn't I the better Jew?" Goldberg asked. "Me?"

After the slightest pause Amos said, "Yes."

Goldberg drew himself back. "I expected maybe an argument." Amos shook his head. "A discussion?" Amos shook his head again. "I was?" Goldberg turned and the ramp started him off. "I was! I really was," he said and left.

Two men in Elizabethan costume arrived. "I'll take over," G1 said, and Amos nodded, slipped past G2 and left the console, rejoining the others behind.

Before the high desk, the First Elizabethan complained. "I am in Debt, great Debt—to *him.*"

The Second Elizabethan said, "Well?" To G1 he said, "Sirrah, at least I'm not carrying a club anymore. And he's not my actual slave. It is 1597, m'Lord."

"By which you mean that you have graduated from mutual extermination and servitude to reciprocal exploitation?" G1 said, his question being a statement.

"Precisely. Is it not Progress?"

"When I owe you a Pound of Flesh?," asked the First Elizabethan.

"Hold it!" Amos cried from below. "Not just after Goldberg. Come on, that's Shylock-ism. From a Shakespeare play, a year or so before."

"You're criticizing—William Shakespeare?" G2 asked.

"Listen—don't be startled—we said before—there are different prisons. Also *times*, which are also confining. For ye crying out loud, there was *bear* baiting on the way to the Globe Theater. He had to compete with that. It explains a lot of the violence, and some of the insensitivity. Nobody writes for all time—"

"No?" G1 asked.

"Not *first* of all," Amos said. "He was, like anybody, *in* his time, not fully free of it. That accounts for the anti-Semitism."

G2 nodded and said to G1, "He's right, you know."

"I know," G1 admitted. "Didn't we just have him up here, in training?"

"All right." G1 turned back fully to the First Elizabethan. "No more similes, please—or recently fashionable quotes."

"The end of the matter being, to put a fine point on it," the First said, "I owe him 500 quid, or the Mortgage on my shoppe."

"So," G1 said to the Second Elizabethan, "you have the advantage of him. If not grasped by the arm or the neck, you have him on the hip. Eh?"

"An historical Process, m'Lord. Business is business is slavery is slow instead of instant murder."

"How exalted," G1 observed. "Change places!" They did. "Now you owe *him* that quid. *Pro quo…* Now, what is he?"

"A usurious Bastard," answered the Second, "full of piss and gall—"

"Yes, yes—and you?"

"A poor—wretch."

"But deep—inside—you're better, you're more than that?"

"I'm a—Person."

"Oh. And he?"

Glancing sheepishly at the First, the Second Elizabethan said, "A person. Possibly. Probably."

"Not either of you," G1 went on, "is an object for slaughter, slavery, mutual exploitation?"

"No," the First said.

"There's something else," said the Second.

G1 asked, "What?"

"We don't know," they answered.

"Get thee hence then." They moved off, as an Australian Woman approached next. "Hence, *hence*," G1 shoo'd them off, "keep hencing, you two."

G2 asked the halted Australian Woman, "Yes? Question?" The Woman shook her head. "Statement?"

The Woman shook her head again. "Revelation," she said.

"Declare time and place."

"New South Wales—our upland Range house. A wide lawn all about. Sunny day. I am a child of six or seven years. My father lies full length, slumbering in the grass. I sit nearby. My dad's hair is flaxen, glinting in the sunshine. Then—"

"What?" G2 asked softly.

"—two birds… alight on his head, his hair. I know now that they want to select strands for their nest. He stirs slightly. They fly away. I never told him; of course, I realize now, I never quite *knew* what to say to anyone, what had even happened. But at the moment, anyway, two birds of the sky flew trustingly into the tangled gold nature of my father. Nothing later in my life matched the peace and beauty of that passing remarkable moment."

"Yes. Of course," G2 said. The Woman turned unceremoniously and left. "Congratulations," G2 called after her.

The assorted lights blipped slowly out, as the ramp bore the Woman away. G2 and G1 slowly wheeled about again.

Chapter 8

"Old chap, why didn't you take a squint," Willie asked Amos, "at the record and… itinerary… up there?"

Maxine said, "He was too honest."

"I was too inflated by my own sense of importance," Amos declared.

"See?" Maxine said.

"Well," Cyrus allowed, "he was pretty good, a regular expert."

"Rather," Willie said.

Something occurred to Amos suddenly. "Say—maybe *that's* it. I mean, back on earth: suppose we were all qualified experts, in a way." To Cyrus he said, "You especially, with your fishing."

"Oh, I—"

"No false modesty… And me as a stand-up comic." He looked at Willie next. "And up to 'utter frustration'—even including it, for all we know—his amorous athletics; oh, and that larceny." Amos pointed at Maxine. "And she painted—" he looked up all at once, as if getting a message—"and won—somehow I know—a South American water color prize." Then he looked toward Phoebe. "And she was, supposedly, just a housewife; but there are housewives and housewives—"

"She was—expert," Cyrus reported.

"So!... Don't you see? Maybe, after all, we're going to some kind of reward for moderate excellence."

"I would never have thought quite that," Maxine said. She concentrated on the idea now, however, musingly. "One's defects and shortcomings stay on one's mind."

"Yep," Cyrus agreed. "I generally forget about that bass on the sugar cube hook. But I always remember the ones that got away, like the big grayling."

"Sure," Amos was also mulling things over. "I got through life not killing anybody—except myself maybe—and yet what often fills my mind is the thought, 'I never saved anybody,' like—"he glanced at Phoebe—"from drowning, or something."

Willie confessed, "I always wanted to find—at least look for—a lost dog. I never did."

Cyrus abruptly asked G1, "Why were trout attracted to treble-hooked fishing lures?"

"They weren't. They were angered by them."

"That's what I figured—and why I always wanted to have them banned!" Cyrus said. "*Why* didn't I do anything about it, in the F and G Association and so forth?"

Coyly Phoebe volunteered, "All I secretly *wished* for, once or twice, was that they would stop using those cute little monkeys for our polio cures and things like that."

"I did nothing—*nada*—to stop, or protest, bullfighting," Maxine said.

After a pause, Amos was still insistent. "But don't you get it? We did as well as possible—and in our hearts—because we still in all had hearts!—we *yearned* as well as we could, as right as we could… Maybe now we're in a way station going to someplace where they don't have lost dogs, false lures, big-eyed rhesus monkeys, violent ritual games with great lurching animal bodies—"

"No human bodies either," Willie interjected. "Personally, I've had enough of flesh! I've been an appendage to my appendage. Enough. As to the whole question, I want dis-embodiment; crave it, in fact. The final expansion, purity—to be space, not matter. The exultation of nothingness!"

"Yeah," Amos said. "That exultation part, though—it doesn't go with the nothing."

Cyrus sidled away from the group toward the central console. "May I claim a… Confidence?" G1 and G2 nodded assent. "I'm secretly afraid—no, that's too strong—a word I never used: wary—wary of—" he inclined his head toward Willie Downs.

"—an intense spirituality?" G2 asked. Cyrus bobbed his head, yes. "Because it's too close to the unspiritual intensity of before."

"You took the thought right out of my head."

"Do you still desire female companionship?" G1 asked.

"Yep," Cyrus said.

"You're somewhat selfish," G1 said.

"Maybe."

"And you're worried by this fanaticism," G2 said, pointing at Willie Downs.

"Or sudden poetic *up*surge," G1 said.

"Please," Cyrus responded, "even if this is in confidence."

"Mr. Wells," G1 told him, "actually, you're a selfish prig."

After the slightest pause, Cyrus cupped his hand to his ear. "Pardon?…"

"A sort of prude," G2 answered quickly.

"Oh. Yes. I can live with it." His own expression made Cyrus self-conscious. "Manner of speaking," he said, glancing at the walls and then back to G1 and G2. "I don't want to exaggerate, you understand, but I *was* an expert fisherman—and deep inside me, against lures, remember. And, outside of me, I tried rescuing youngsters from downtown Minneapolis. And—"

"We know, we know," G1 interrupted. "That's quite unnecessary. You're basically all right."

"Even if you're worried by that Englishman," G2 added.

"I don't hate him, mind you. I don't hate anybody here."

"Neither do the others," G1 said.

"I just wonder if you'd tell me whether he'll wind up with—" Cyrus looked toward the women.

"No," G2 replied with momentary ambiguity, "no, we won't tell you."

Cyrus accepted that and returned to the others. Maxine was talking to Amos and Phoebe about Willie, since no time had elapsed.

"I understand his craving for spirituality. He mentioned purity. It's like the release of sainthood. Personally, I am not ready for the completeness of it, but I understand."

"Hold it," Amos said, "I can't agree with that. I'm in no mood to go someplace where I won't have this funny but familiar body." He looked from one woman to another. "I need to feel breezes, all right—and the air conditioning. I think I *do* feel it." He hugged himself. "Body, body—oh, the gravity of the situation... Otherwise," he let go, "I quit."

"You can't quit," Phoebe said.

"No?" Amos looked rapidly from her to G1 and G2, neither of whom responded.

"So," Maxine prompted Amos further, "you loved the breeze, too?"

"Absolutely. And walking on the beach. And smelling fir trees, and—" he remembered something else—"a drink of water... Listen, I visited a guy who had a house in Northern California, off by itself in some woods and mountains, and he had well water. It was delicious!" He turned to Willie. "By our time we had cars and flying machines and rockets to the moon, but you could live and die and never know what a natural drink of water tasted like." G1 held up two fingers at him. Amos was baffled. "What is that, V for Victory?"

"No," G1 said, "for two: the two-ness of everything."

"Extraordinary," Willie said. "Things got better *and* worse? More marvelous... and deteriorated?" He reflected a moment. "Perhaps that was already somewhat true in my day."

"Anyway," Maxine said to Amos, "you liked the wind, a clear drink of water—"

"Yes," Amos said, going to the buffet once more, activating his memory as he talked and inspected the laden table. "And favorite food to eat. Not just special cherry cheese cake. All kinds of ordinary food."

The others approached the buffet with him, avidly looking for what they named, for what re-occurred to them all at once.

"A good Denver omelet," Cyrus said.

"Broiled pompano," Maxine said.

"A Nathan hot dog," Amos added.

"Fresh orange juice," Phoebe looked up briefly. "Before it got so expensive."

"French toast! I say!"

Cyrus remembered further, "Why didn't we know that the bismarcks made at Haugen's bakery in St. Paul, when we were young, weren't forever? When Mr. Haugen died, so did they. You could get cream-filled or even jelly-filled doughnuts somewhere else, but not like that. How come someone didn't tell us that the particular good thing in front of us wasn't for all time—so we could taste it *more*?"

"And Swenson's ice cream parlor," Phoebe recalled, "the chocolate sundae."

Willie said, "I wanted chocolate *any* day."

"Or just hot morning coffee from *Brasil*," Maxine said.

Phoebe sat at one of the small tables nearby. "Or duck lichée." Maxine, Willie, and Cyrus joined her.

"Nope," Amos said. His mock self-importance was also serious. "This is ordinary, not highfalutin. You can have chop suey, not duck lichée."

"I don't like chop suey."

Amos' seriousness slipped back into comic charade. He took a napkin from the buffet table and draped it over one arm as a waiter's towel. "I've got egg foo yong. And a simple crisp egg roll."

Phoebe shook her head. "Duck lichée."

"I can even give you bird's nest soup, won ton but no—"

"Duck lichée."

"Water chestnuts, sweet-and-sour—"

Phoebe was obstinate. "Duck lichée."

G2 broke in with a question. "Wasn't that quite common in Canton?"

"Oh?" Amos said. "I see! Peking Duck was a capital item only in Peking; everywhere else it was—"he held up an ordering hand and index finger to G1—"one duck lichée for the lady from Minnesota!" He took off the napkin and walked back to the buffet.

"Thank you," Phoebe called after him.

With a prestigious motion toward the buffet table, G1 said: "It's there. Whenever she wants it… Whatever anybody wants."

"Except lobster," Maxine called out. "I hope no one will order or even think of it. No *live* lobster cooking."

"No," they answered, severally, "Hear, hear!" and also, "That's right!" and "Agreed."

"And you agree also," G1 asked, "no dried blood."

There was an instant chorus. "What did he say?" "Ugh!" "Did I hear right?" "Unbelievable." "What happened to him?"

"Just proving a point," G1 said. "Your combined abhorrence of the Chinese favorite, dried blood, is matched only by their disgust for your consumption of milk—which, to them, was almost like urine."

"I won't believe it," Phoebe said.

G1 bowed toward her. "Madame. It was—is—a varied cosmos. Especially your mid-way earth. Very interesting, in an astronomical and biocultural sense. Take cannibalism—"

There was general dismay, repulsion.

"Anachronistically, he means," G2 said.

G1 made a slight, courtly bow to G2 also. "Quite so. A man consumed his foe: an act of destruction *and* incorporation. He ate his brain for wisdom, his heart for courage, his—"

"Don't go on," Willie said.

"I simply mean, it was inextricably the worst and best of worlds right from the start, and it will be so to proceed and end with." G1 made the V sign again. "Two-in-one. Always."

Amos was struck by something. He sauntered over closer to the others. "You know what? Einstein was still alive when I was a kid. In other words, I lived on earth for a while between Einstein and—Tupperware parties."

"Tupperware parties?" Maxine asked.

"Some things can't be translated," Amos said.

G1 said, "It was certainly absurd. Ambiguous."

Maxine asked, "Are we headed for something less—"

"—absurd?" G2 anticipated.

"—ambiguous?" Maxine asked.

"Always that, no matter what," G1 declared. "But we don't quite know all the next higher or even parallel worlds."

"You don't?" Amos said. He poked Maxine gently. "And I thought they were god at least with a little g."

Phoebe Wells spoke up. "But just where are we going, the five of *us*? Can't we find that out?"

"But Miss Nightingale—"G1 started to say.

G2 looked at G1 abruptly. "Miss? They can review, even revise a trifle, but not revert."

"Missus then?" G1 tried. "Or: *Miz*. Everything's in flux, even here." To Phoebe, G1 said directly, "The point is, how can you know exactly or comprehensively where you're going until you've been there?"

Amos fumbled in mockery at a pocket for a non-existent pen and pad. "Let me write that down, please. Yes sir, that suggests a *lot* less than it says."

Cyrus Wells was serious in appeal to G1 and G2. "Won't you tell us at least what direction we're headed in?"

"Somewhere perhaps higher on the scale?" Maxine asked.

Although they did not answer directly, G1 and G2 exchanged glances with one another.

"Some indication, at this juncture, just conceivably in their intellectual range?" G2 suggested.

G1 turned to the areaway, where two vastly cloaked and hooded figures appeared simultaneously as he spoke. "That means the Heizinger Quadrant, the paralactical Intersect through cube-curve at Cymbelos: no more than an earth-timed minute of sub-intense intellectual radiation…"

The cloaked and hooded figures, featureless and practically bodiless within the folds of their outsized hoods and robes, came forward to a point somewhat above but between the high console desk and the group of five. The two halted and conferred aloud. Their voices were deliberate, deep, even sepulchral, but also calm, resonant, meditative.

"Say: S1 for the System, is the log of K," the first figure theorized. "Then Entropy is the log of the number of independent possibilities."

"Therefore Entropy is directly related to Evolution?" mused the second. "More randomness, or disorder, will be associated with higher structures—everywhere?"

"To preserve the constancy of systems."

"Also suggesting that imperfection is a corollary of mutation. Similarly, independence and elaboration."

"Leading to some ultimate Depository as enormous and superior and paradoxical as to have outgrown early developmental origins, incapable of understanding and consciously regulating them anymore—"

"—as bio-structural entities are to their autonomic processes—"

They turned away, to leave.

"—like ourselves, mentally and temporally so far along as to have forgotten how it began."

"Was it the leap from hydrogen to helium?"

The first figure reached the areaway again and left. The second, still speculating, was trailing slightly after.

"There probably wasn't even three-space originally, but two-space fragmented into a whole other dimension, with so much more space than matter…"

The deep, resonating voices ceased. The figures were gone.

"Was that on a high enough scale for you, Max?" Amos asked.

Phoebe cut in. "Did you understand?"

"Almost," Amos answered.

"Will you explain it to me… sometime?"

"Sure," Amos promised, "if I haven't forgotten by then. And, if I have, I'll explain it anyway."

Willie Downs had been pondering. "Then there isn't a God?"

"Or either there is and there won't be," Cyrus said. "Or there will be and there wasn't."

After studying Cyrus momentarily, Maxine said, "That's quite close to what I thought."

"It makes you lonely, though," Amos remarked.

"Maybe," Phoebe said, 'that's why there are two of even *them*."

Maxine smiled at Phoebe in acknowledgment. "G1 *and* G2," she pointed to the console. "And two and two among us, except for one extra who is—"

Amos felt threatened: "—superfluous?"

Cyrus felt trapped: "—self-sufficient?"

Willie felt grateful: "—impelled to the stars, toward monasteries of compact light."

"Heavy, heavy," Amos said. "Let's get back down to earth. I mean, well…" He turned to Maxine. "You were lonely, too? Are?"

From the console G1 intoned, "Yes, start sorting yourselves out."

"It's almost time," seconded G2.

Amos pressed Maxine. "How about a beautiful Peruvian painter going off with a comic nincompoop?"

"You're *not* a nincompoop."

"Careful! The next thing you'll say is I'm not comic. Come on, Max, let me save your next life. Let's grab a sunbeam to Heizinger or Cymbelos… What do you say?"

"You're lovely, Amos, adorable…"

"I'm lovely, adorable. But."

"And you're manly."

"Manly?" Amos was skeptical but already mollified. "*How?*"

"You're brave inside here," Maxine tapped Amos' head. "That's really manly."

"I'm lovely. I'm adorable. I'm manly. But I'm not engaged." He walked away. He spoke to G1 and G2. "So, I feel—"

"Aggressive," G2 understood. "Violent."

"Damn right."

"On a good night," G1 said, "you used to 'kill' whole audiences."

"You liked being a 'riot,' remember?" G2 prompted him.

"Yes."

"Did you happen to know," G1 asked in his general offhand pertinence, "that 'man slaughter' and 'man's laughter' were spelled exactly the same?"

Struck by that, Amos said, "My God! I was a highly sublimated being." He looked in turn at each of the others. "And Willie, you spent actual time in jail. And Max, you were artistically ruthless on a lot of occasions. So were you, Cyrus. And, Phoebe, let's not go into *all* your dream life… For 'nice' people, we—hey!" he said to G1, "All right, not Heaven then—there, here, or wherever—but the other?"

"Both!" G1 maintained. "It's always both, in one degree or another, everywhere."

"Don't give us everywhere! Are we headed up, down, or sideways, or what? *Where?*"

G1 shrugged. "A realm of possibilities. You're talking about n to the sixteenth power. The best any of us can do is make an inspired guess."

"So make it," Amos said.

"Oh, we've made it," G2 chimed in. "We won't quite share it, yet. Perhaps, as you leave—in the long sidereal corridor—" G2 pointed to the areaway and beyond— "out there—you yourselves will divine it." G2 asked G1 suddenly, "Do you think they're ready?"

"Almost. But one more—"G1 lifted an arm to the ramp door—"demonstration." The ramp moved, lights and sounds blipped and bleeped. G1 and G2 turned about to greet the entrants, and the five below waited with tense curiosity.

Chapter 9

Two cockaded French Revolutionaries approached the console desk.

The First Revolutionary said, "We're from 'hence' with an answer. *The* answer."

"What is it?" G1 asked.

The Second Revolutionary put his arms around the shoulders of the First, who reciprocated. They both said, "Tolerance!"

"Live and let live?" G2 asked.

"Liberty," said the First Revolutionary.

"Equality," said the Second.

"And Fraternity," G2 said or recited. "Yes. But there's more yet than tolerance." The two Revolutionaries were alert. "One might even actively *help* the other one out." The two nodded happily.

"There is a higher stage yet," G1 said. The faces of the Revolutionaries, as G1 recapitulated, registered surprise, doubt, hope, then expectation. "Not only do you no longer destroy the other—or enslave, exploit, manipulate, or use him—or merely tolerate or even help him—but you may *appreciate* him."

"Or her, as the case may be," G2 said.

"Oh," the First Revolutionary said, grappling with the concept, not gender.

"Yes," said the Second.

They took off their cockade hats and put on, perhaps from a lower recess in the high console, modern head-ware. They started to move off along the ramp.

"Wait," G1 halted them. "There's a further answer. You can assimilate what's different, take it into yourself—French grace, Italian warmth, Irish wit, Jewish humor, Dutch order, Japanese delicacy, et cetera. Beyond tolerance—mutual appreciation, cultivation." The two nodded vigorously, somewhere found two more hats, futuristic ones, exchanging them for the others, and resumed leave-taking again. "Wait! There's more, there must be."

"What?" they asked.

G2 answered. "We don't know. Take off all hats." They did. "Clear the head. Think for yourself." The Revolutionaries now definitely moved off along the sliding ramp. "You're on your own now."

A white-jacketed Scientist approached after them. She stood before G1 and G2 with shoulders squared and hands pushed stiffly into her smock pockets.

"My work on the centipede," she asked: "detaching and reversing the front fifty legs, so that it walked against itself, nowhere—"

"My word!" Willie exclaimed. He turned to Cyrus. "But it might have made jolly good bait…?"

"I don't care," Cyrus replied, "throw her out!"

Imperturbably the Scientist finished her question. "—it proved what?"

Amos said, "Unbelievable."

"You can say that again," Maxine said.

"Unbelievable," Amos duly said. Then he was serious. "That wouldn't make it any more acceptable," he said.

"I know one thing," the Scientist persisted, "that it proved the lower cells are not directly controlled by the higher. But ultimately? in the scheme of things—?"

"It means," said G1, "there is no overall control."

And that was all of that last Procession. The Woman Scientist left, the sliding ramp carrying her off and whirring to a stop, the winking lights and bleeping sounds trembling off.

Chapter 10

"But what about the centipede?" Cyrus asked.

"Ingenious experiment," G1 commented, "technically speaking."

"Rum show for the centipede," Willie said, "and I never particularly liked centipedes, actually."

Amos groaned. "*When* are we all going to get our act together?"

"A good question," G2 said. "*The* good question. And since you asked," G2 turned ceremoniously to G1 "they're ready now. It's time."

G1 stamped some documents on the console desk, five distinct times. The group shuffled more or less toward the desk to receive papers. "Oh, I haven't anything for you… You've gotten what you need… Goodbye, cheerio, *hasta la vista.*"

"And we really mean—*vista,*" G2 added.

Willie barely touched two fingers to his forehead as an informal salute to G1 and G2. Then, in rapid succession, he shook hands with each of the others in turn. "Goodbye, old chaps." Although he was visibly affected—or because he was—he left abruptly, walking briskly up to and then through the areaway.

Looking after him, G2 said at last, "He was really quite nice. I hope he—"

"Well, he's in *some* sort of transport by now," G1 said.

Amos shook Maxine's hand, holding it for a prolonged moment as he looked into her eyes. "I really 'appreciate' you; I got that far anyway. So long, Max." He turned quickly to the Wellses.

All at once Phoebe kissed Cyrus on the check. "Bye, Cyrus… I think we should have *talked* more. I—" she turned from him swiftly and shook Maxine's hand and headed out before her. "You want to wait for me?" she called ahead to Amos, "if you don't—"

"—mind? No!" Amos said, stopping. "No… I—er—hope you didn't mind that passing infatuation," he indicated Maxine behind them.

"Oh, I had one, too," Phoebe said, inclining her head in the other direction. "I understand."

Before leaving with her, Amos indicated her costume and asked, "Maybe we could get you a jacket or something?"

"I'm not cold at all, thank you." Phoebe spied the deck of cards left on one of the tables. "Maybe we can take them with us." She scooped them together, while Amos had a second thought about the buffet.

"I'll grab bagel and lox for the trip. And I think," he said, looking quickly into and then closing and picking up a box, "they boxed your duck lichée." They proceeded out together, but on the threshold of departure, Amos halted and turned around for one final survey of the Terminal. "Like the man says, I feel a hell of a lot more like I do now than when we first came in."

He turned around again, as Phoebe laughed. And they left together.

G1 faced G2. "She and Amos Kidderly? Pairing off like that?"

"Perhaps, unknown to him, he responds in part to the mothering still in her," G1 said.

"And he had what Willie Downs didn't for her—devotion, under all the comedy... They may work out very well."

Both G1 and G2 fixed their gaze on Maxine and Cyrus.

"Well, then," Maxine said simply. "Could I, I wonder, paint... some new kind of Norway... with you?"

They nodded at G1 and G2 and sedately left.

"Well," G2 observed, "that pair at least had nature in common."

"I daresay," G1 said.

"They were *all* quite nice, finally," G2 said. "Wherever they're going." She looked expectantly, steadily at G1.

"Just elsewhere," G1 replied. "I don't know very much more than you on this assignment... It's just elsewhere, onward—quite as we said, for the few who *really* want to... To be perfectly candid, there's the other point of view that interests me: not whether there's life after death, but truly, life *before* death."

"Yes," G2 agreed. She held herself, all at once, feeling her arms. "I should like to stay... embodied... just now."

"Oh?"

"Why were we swathed like this?"

"Awe. A certain amount of awe, heightened by familiarity—though the awe was wearing off somewhat."

"These are lovely... structures... underneath, don't you agree?"

"Well," G1 said, "I haven't actually been too—conscious—of—"

"We could... furlough... like this, couldn't we?" G2 asked, seductively. "After Intermediary Duty. A million-year afternoon, or evening. Wouldn't you—?"

"All right... Which half would you like to be?"

"Oh," G2 ran her hands along her arms once more, gliding them to her cleavage and breasts. "I think I'll take *this* part."

She disengaged the codpiece, as G1 did the ballet skirt. They came around and down either end of the desk chairs.

"Do you hear the music?" G1 asked.

There was perfect silence, but G2 pirouetted for G1's full inspection and approval and her own sensuous enthusiasm.

"Isn't it... lovely?"

G1 looked at all of her. "Oh yes." They danced together in a wide circuit. He stepped back a trifle, as he held her. "I like the shape of your soul."

They danced on.

"Oh dear," G2 said presently, "my head is spinning." They stopped. They pulled and unwound their head bandages, revealing good-looking, very pleasant faces. "This is closer to the soul yet," she remarked, and they danced some more. "I must say, I knew the mistakes, the volatility, extended to us, too—"

"The Entropy factor," G1 declared.

"May I tell you in language—"

"Of course."

"—that I have enjoyed your evolving—"

"—forthrightness?"

"Yes. And I have liked your—"

"—independence?" G1 asked.

"Decidedly."

"And thank you for thinking so many of my thoughts."

They were still dancing.

"Not at all."

They halted temporarily, as she put her fingers gently on his face.

"I also like the touching part," G2 said. They resumed their slow ballet. "Oh, I could go on like this for—"

"—just as long as you like," G1 said. "Just as long as... we... like."

Made in the USA
Middletown, DE
31 December 2020

30513291R00040